IN SEARCH OF LOVE

IN SEARCH OF LOVE

Helen McCabe

CHIVERS

British Library Cataloguing in Publication Data available

This Large Print edition published by BBC Audiobooks Ltd, Bath, 2010.
Published by arrangement with the Author.

U.K. Hardcover ISBN 978 1 408 45788 7
U.K. Softcover ISBN 978 1 408 45789 4

Printed and bound in Great Britain by
CPI Antony Rowe, Chippenham and Eastbourne

CHAPTER ONE

1903

Mary would never forget the first time she saw Sean Mullen from Kerry. He seemed strangely familiar to her and it was only a few short months later that he became the man who strode through her dreams, haunting her nightly.

That April morning, she and her friend, Bridie, desperate to get out of the sickly atmosphere that prevailed in their cramped quarters below deck, had taken their lives in their hands and climbed up the ship's ladder, skirts blowing, to brave the fierce gale and the rain, which was driving the vessel mercilessly on across the Atlantic Ocean towards a new world for both of them.

Sean was pulling on to a stout rope for a few pence, like he'd been born to a seafaring life. Mary's quick, young eyes glanced sideways taking in the sight of his taut body exposed to the elements.

'Look at him,' Bridie whispered, 'he is like a part of the wind itself.' As virtuous women, they should have averted their gaze, but both were too excited.

'Shame on you, Bridie,' mouthed Mary, holding on to her hat, which the mad gale was trying to rip off. At that very moment, she caught Sean's impudent, appraising glance and, without another look at him, she grabbed Bridie by the arm and, together, they fought their way over to the rail to see if they could get their first glance of America.

Ellis Island, New York.

'Do you still believe your aunt will come to fetch you?' Bridie asked.

Mary looked up from the shirt seam she was sewing. 'I'm sure she will,' she replied. She had a determined look about her, that showed in the angle of her chin, which was dimpled with a pretty cleft. Inside, she was not feeling that confident, but she didn't want her friend to know how upset she was about what had happened. She was on her own now and she had to be strong!

'How can you bear it?' Bridie asked. She had received the letter she had been waiting for only two days ago and she'd been happy ever since. She watched her friend pityingly struggling with her needle and the heavy material.

The serge you had to sew and mend, made your fingers hurt and most of the women had sore hands after days and days of sewing. That was why Bridie was so happy about her letter. Her cousin Pat was coming at last to pick her up from Ellis Island. It was a long journey to the farm in Connecticut, where he worked and she was only going to be the female help, but she would have gone to the ends of the earth to get away from here, where they had been stuck for weeks.

She looked at her own handiwork for the day. All hers! She'd been allowed to finish the hem of the first new skirt she'd had for years. It had been bought for her by 'The Contingency Fund'. Such big words, hard to say and hard to write. Bridie had hardly any book learning and had to sign her name with a cross! But her friend Mary Flynn was very bright, could read anything, and had done all the letter writing for most of the others. And now Mary was to be left behind. It wasn't fair at all!

She looked across at Mary, who was leaning over her work as if she had nothing else on her mind. Pretty and brave, her dark curls tumbled over her shoulders. She also had the deepest blue eyes Bridie had ever seen . . .

Mary glanced up to see the pitying expression on Bridie's face. No one must ever know how much her mind was in a turmoil. She had met Bridie on board ship on their passage from Cork and the girls, although entirely different in character, had become the greatest friends.

So she looked up and hid the sadness she was feeling by a brave expression. She determined to be sunny enough even to make

Mr McLeish chuckle. He was the dour old Scottish supervisor who was in charge of the women and children of all nationalities, who were waiting to be claimed.

Sometimes it surprised Mary that she could make him laugh. 'Och, ye're as bonny as a blackbird, Mary Flynn. May good luck come your way soon!' But it hadn't so far . . .

In spite of trying to be happy for Bridie, Mary's smile was very different from the one she had worn when she'd first arrived on Ellis Island. Then she'd been hopeful. Now she was losing that brightness of spirit. To her horror, she could feel tears pricking behind her eyelids.

'Why are you looking at me like that, Bridie,' Mary burst out passionately to cover her distress. 'Sure I'm not dead yet!'

'How am I looking?' Bridie asked timidly. Mary could show her temper sometimes. Not that Bridie blamed her.

'Like you're sorry for me,' Mary snapped. Of course her friend was sorry for her. Who wouldn't be? She'd been on Ellis Island for three whole months and there still had been no word from Auntie Flynn, who was her father's only sister and who had promised to pick up Mary once she had been pronounced fit and well to enter America.

But she'd let Mary down and the girl didn't know why. Mary sniffed quietly. Her dear father had died when she was 15 and she'd

4

been the rock that her mother had leaned on in that awful year following his death. Then Thomas Odone had turned up. He was the coachman at the Big House in the village and also a widower looking for another wife. He purported to have been good friends with her father, but Mary was not sure about that.

Dadda had never spoken of him in pleasant terms and Mary was sure that he would have hated the thought that Odone had taken over his home and family. But the marriage had been approved by the owners of the Big House and Thomas had wed her mother who, Mary knew, was finding it very hard to make ends meet.

So, before she turned 17, Mary had found herself with a stepfather—and one she could not trust. She especially hated the way he looked at her with his narrow eyes. She lived in fear that one night he would come in to her bedroom, instead of pausing outside. She always trembled when she heard the tread of his heavy boots on the stairs. Mary shivered as she remembered . . .

However, although Mary would have wished that her dearest mother had found herself a different husband, Thomas seemed to treat her well and that was, for Mary, the most important thing in the world.

Then her night prayers had been heard. Auntie Flynn had written to her mother to say that now Mary was grown she would be very welcome to join her in New York, where she had emigrated with her husband, Danny.

Aunt Flynn's husband had now died and she was running a boarding house as a business. *Very small it is*, she'd written, *and I have only one tiny room free. But Mary will be welcome and I will be glad of her company and her help.*

A lump came up in Mary's throat as she remembered the last farewell with her mother standing wrapped in her shawl, waving her goodbye from the shore. It had seemed that the whole boat had been crying, but many on it had little to cry for because they were leaving Ireland.

Life had been getting harder all the time as new landlords took over, but the Flynn family was well known in their village and were favoured by Lady Bennett at the Big House, which had been the seat of an English gentleman for a long time. Why the Flynns were the lady's favourites, Mary never really knew, but it was a fact that was accepted in the neighbourhood and not ever spoken of.

The lady herself was Irish-born and from an aristocratic well-set up family, whereas Lord Bennett was an Englishman who had held a minor seat in government. Evidently his family had not been too pleased when their son had married an Irish girl, but it was her father's wealth that had finally convinced them. Mary often thought Lady Bennett seemed unhappy, with her drawn, white face and sad dark eyes, but she never knew how anyone could be with such a lovely home and everything she wanted in the world. And if any of the old ones in the village knew they never spoke openly of it, for fear of losing their livelihood. But there were whispers . . . So Mary was often sent for by Lady Bennett to come over to the great house and read to her.

Dadda had taught Mary to read and write well; he was book-learned and came from a family of farmers, most of whose land had been taken over by an unscrupulous English landlord, causing him to become only a tenant with a tiny holding. Over 20 years ago, he had moved to their present home in the West to work for the rich folks, who were the ruling squires of Brala.

He could tell both bitter and beautiful stories of Ireland's past and Mary had grown up with the deeds of High Kings and Queens as well as a deep knowledge of the great potato famine. Mary had often wished that he would tell her the story and how he had finally come to be in Brala, but on that he was silent.

Dadda was strong in body and spirit and, in spite of his hard life, he always had a winsome smile on his handsome face as well as a charming word for everyone that he met. He became the Bennetts' head gardener. Mary's mother had told her that Lady Bennett had always liked Dadda's good humour and had made sure that he spent most of his time planning and tilling her extensive gardens, which he managed to combine with his sea fishing. With the two jobs, the four cows and their three donkeys, they'd managed to save a little money. But, then Dadda had died . . .

When the letter came from Aunt Margaret Flynn, Mary had realised she would never be able to afford to go. And, even if she did have the money, it didn't seem right to leave her mother.

Then, to her great astonishment, Odone had come home one night with some amazing news. He had been called into the servants' parlour by Lady Bennett, who had heard about Mary's offer from her Aunt Flynn.

'As a token of esteem in memory of her dear father, my faithful servant, I, personally, will be pleased to pay the girl's passage. It is what Conor Flynn would have wanted for his daughter, if he'd lived. It is a great opportunity for Mary. And she's a bright girl. She has pleased me so many times with her reading,' the lady had told him.

Mary had been overjoyed. When she went to thank her, Lady Bennett had smiled graciously with a, 'Yes, yes, run away, child.' But Mary could see she had been moved by the gesture. In fact, there was a brightness in her eyes, which Mary took for tears. It was all very strange! Poor Lord and Lady Bennett had no children of their own.

And so that was how a very poor Mary had

managed to arrive on Ellis Island, having set sail for America from her native shores in the Spring of 1903.

Mary put down the shirt she was sewing and stared at the seam with dry, shining eyes. She was determined not to cry now. That, she did in the privacy of her little bed. She had not come across the world to give up, she told herself firmly. She would find a way to stay here and prosper, and also track down her Aunt Flynn. On the other hand, she was trapped. She couldn't get off the island without someone coming to fetch her.

'One day, Bridie, you'll see. You'll be on your way to Connecticut and, soon afterwards, Auntie Flynn will come walking through that door.' If she said it enough times she might believe it herself . . . Just then the bell was rung, which signified the end of another dreary working day.

Later as Mary knelt in prayer, she was turning over ideas in her head instead of concentrating on her prayers. She raised her head slightly and glanced through the window, to where the moonlight shone on the sea, making it silver.

She knew it was only a short boat ride to the New York shore. She'd stared over enough times to that enormous huddle of buildings, which were rising and encroaching on more land every day as the mighty city grew and burst its seams, hardly able to accommodate

9

the thousands of people who sought their freedom in the New World.

She could even row over there herself! It was only a sea river and she and her father had braved the edge of the storms coming off the Atlantic often in their tiny fishing boat when they'd been setting their creels in the bay back home.

But sensible Mary also knew that it was actually as far as the moon and there was no hope of her doing it, because regular patrols swept the waters around Ellis Island to make sure no one had the same idea as she—of getting over to the New York shore before permission had been granted.

Indeed, she might as well have been in prison! But the great red building where they were being held was not a gaol. In fact, they were all treated kindly and fairly. Thousands had passed through its doors already to find a new and better life and the only people who were sent back were those who were incurably ill or feeble in mind, which seemed harsh. Also anyone who was not claimed or could not be found a decent situation.

So far, Mary was one of the latter. It was easier for the men to find work as the authorities wanted labourers, but they would not let unmarried girls go to just anyone who offered, in case they fell into evil hands!

It was all so frustrating. Mary had passed all the tests she had been set. She remembered how afraid she had been when she'd arrived in the Great Hall where the officers sat at their high desks ready to interrogate every single soul, man, woman and child. Then men, women and children had been separated, divided into separate columns and all of them had wearily climbed the massive staircase to file into a series of small rooms where each person was examined.

Mary had been prodded by a nurse, then poked by a doctor, who peered into her eyes, rolled the lids back on a matchstick to look for any signs of disease, then stared down her throat. Afterwards, he felt her all over just like Dadda felt the horses and donkeys at the annual summer fair.

Afterwards, she'd been made to sit and draw animals and birds; to name them and other pictures; to write, count and build puzzles. She knew it was to find out if she was a simpleton. But she had little to be afraid of because she had always been quick to learn, unlike many of the women and children who were waiting their turn. Mary came from an unusual family—one with determination!

In fact, it had all been very easy for Mary. Yet she had never seen so many different people, all herded together; Jews, Russians, Poles; all speaking unintelligible languages; all determined to get into America!

Mary had passed all her tests. 'Very well!' they said. 'You will do well in America.' But, as

11

the days passed and Aunt Flynn did not appear, Mary became less bright and more depressed because she could not understand why she'd been abandoned—and, now, her only close friend, Bridie, was leaving her too.

Mary had written several letters to Aunt Flynn, but she had received no replies. She knew she had to do something—but what? Suddenly, as the prayers were near to finishing, a very bold thought rushed into her head—so bold that it made her cheeks go red hot and her heart race in her chest.

She glanced around, anxious she was giving herself away but everyone else seemed intent on their prayers and appeared not to have noticed her excitement. Half an hour later, as she made her way through a maze of corridors to the dormitory which she shared with the other women, she could hardly wait . . .

As soon as she was sitting on her bed, she drew the threadbare curtains around her to ensure her privacy. Then she slipped her hand into her bodice and withdrew her newest possession, which she had threatened to throw away several times, but hadn't the heart to.

She stared at it frowning but, seconds later, had to smile in spite of her apprehension as to the dangerous course she was thinking of taking. Sean Mullen's roguish brown eyes seemed to be staring into hers, gently mocking her discomfiture.

She turned over the big, flat, wax seal he

had given her and thought deeply. He had scratched the legend on it with a short knife, which he'd assured her he kept for safety. He had said other things too! Suddenly, Mary was tremendously glad that the address hadn't melted with the heat of her skin.

Slowly she stretched out her hand for the fine pen and ink she had been saving for any emergency. Then she rummaged about in the little box where she kept the sheets of paper she'd been saving too. She couldn't see well enough to write the letter now in the dark twilight of the early autumn evening. She would write the actual letter tomorrow and tonight she would think what would be the best thing to say. It was her only chance of escape!

She considered how shameless she'd become, thinking of writing to an unmarried man she hardly knew. The she remembered Bridie's envious words, 'Sean Mullen holds a torch for you!' She'd scoffed at the thought, even giggled, but now Mary was deadly serious. She leaned back against her pillow and stared at the address on the seal.

Sean Mullen, in the care of The Shamrock Tree, 1451 Murtagh Buildings, Down Town, New York.

Privately, Mary had been enchanted by Sean. She'd known very few young men. Her Dadda had seen to that! She'd acquainted herself with one or two of the grooms at the

13

Big House on her business with the hunters, but they were only little lads.

She'd often wondered who Dadda had in mind for her to marry, but neither he nor her mother had ever mentioned the fact. She had only hoped it would not have been one of the old farmers, who were always looking for young wives to do the farm work and bear children.

Mary didn't want to think about the latter. Was that what Mrs O'Toole had meant regarding Sean Mullen? She tried not to think about it, although it always came back into her head. She'd heard many lewd whispers about the doings of men and women since she'd been on Ellis and unprotected by her parents.

I will write to him when it's daylight to say that I need someone to stand and speak for me so that I can get into New York and find Auntie Flynn, she thought determinedly. *I can look after myself and Sean will find that out. If he replies . . .* She wasn't sure what she would do if he did. But it was her only chance; and it could possibly be her last.

As Mary settled down to sleep, suddenly his handsome face came into sharp focus and her mind began to rove back over how she and Sean Mullen had sought each other's company on the ship to America.

CHAPTER TWO

Some time after the girls had seen him hauling on the rope, Sean had made himself known to them and most of the girls on their part of the ship! But he spent most of his time in the vicinity of Mary's quarters, which several women had remarked upon, making Mary's cheeks blaze.

Indeed, he had never been alone with her until that special day she had kept locked in her heart. The rest of the time he had almost driven the girls crazy with his teasing but, in reality, they were glad of anyone to cheer them up as they lived through the hell that was steerage class. Below decks was crammed with far too many people, who seemed to have brought everything they owned with them for their new life in the New World. Farm implements, family heirlooms, trunks filled to overflowing were stacked everywhere while most of the rich folks' things were in the hold to be cared for.

That particularly eventful night—the one before they docked—Sean Mullen pushed his way along the narrow passageway to that part of the ship where Bridie and Mary were lumped up together in a bunk above Mrs O'Toole, who because of her size could never have climbed up on top. He'd been a not unwelcome visitor to that part of the ship since his eyes had lighted on Mary Flynn from Brala, Cork.

'It's you again, Mullen, is it?' Margaret O'Toole hissed.

'Be quiet now, missis,' he replied politely, 'and give me the chance to say goodbye to the girls.' He would rather have told her off, but he was too much of a gentleman. He only pitied the farmer in Ohio who was going to marry her.

'Can you not leave decent, God-fearing folk alone?' she went on. 'We are sick and tired of you and your bragging!'

Mary would have liked to have called out then boldly, 'We are not!' but she didn't dare. She would not a put a foot wrong until that foot was firmly fixed on American shores.

But, just at that moment, Sean Mullen had caught hold of it as it dangled over the edge of the bunk and was stroking her naked toes!

'You have a fine foot, my lady,' he mocked, sweeping her a tiny bow and, all the while, he was softly squeezing them with his strong fingers. A strange feeling like liquid treacle ran through her, but she drew her foot back out of his grasp and sat cross-legged above him staring down into those bold, dark eyes, which she declared to herself, she would never forget until Judgement Day.

'Behave yourself, Sean!' she remonstrated. 'And keep away from my feet in case they deliver you a kick.' Her eyes flashed at the soft mocking in his.

He was reaching up towards her bunk and she moved back quickly. 'I would rather it was a kiss, Mary Flynn,' he whispered and she heard Bridie give a little hiccup of excitement from where she was turned lying to the wall.

'Don't be getting above yourself, Sean Mullen!' she snapped. 'If you do not get down, I'll be calling the man who will put you out.'

'And who will that be?' he countered. Sean thought a lot of himself; of his strength and his wit. But, although he was arrogant, she liked him a lot. She would have given several pennies to hear him sing a sad Irish ballad in that rich tenor of his. The words reminded her so much of home.

'You know who!' By that time, Mrs O'Toole was tugging at the tail of his shirt to make him stop.

'Come down, ye young divil!' she cried, 'or I'll be fetching the purser myself and telling him that you are harassing Christian women!' Next moment, he was standing below with a look on his face that rent Mary's heart.

'I'll be good then, Mrs O'Toole,' he promised. 'And even better if Miss Flynn will take a turn on the lower deck with me.' His eyes twinkled, melting Mary's heart. It was always the same and had been so ever since they had left Cork. Mary swung down her legs and next moment, she was following him.

With Mrs O'Toole's warnings ringing in her ears, and Bridie's envious whispers in her head she and Sean Mullen were soon standing under a hatch, oblivious of the reek and stink of the boat around them. And that was when he had given her the seal.

'What is it?' she asked, when he handed the flat object to her.

'My seal!' he said.

'Yours?' her brow furrowed. There was an inscription around it, which she could hardly make out but, somewhere, something buzzed in her brain. She'd seen something like it before, but where?

'I am descended from high folk,' he quipped, but there was a hard look on his face which she had seen but rarely. Then his expression changed. 'You can keep it,' he said. 'I don't want it. I'll earn myself another in the New World.'

'But what will I do with it?' she asked.

'Why you can stamp all those letters with it that you send home. It will make you look important.' His hand on her elbow made her quiver.

'You're a strange one, Sean Mullen!' she said, to cover her confusion. 'Now why on earth would I want a seal anyway? And as for one of yours . . .'

'Mary,' he said, pulling her closer, 'you'll need it to remember me.'

'Why should I want to remember you?'

18

joked Mary, although the question was very far from the truth. She wanted to desperately.

'Because you like me, Mary Flynn.' She began to pull away, glancing around anxiously in case anyone heard. But no one in that wild mass of people were taking notice. 'I know you do and because . . .' He seemed stuck for words, which too was very rare. 'Would you like to be my sweetheart?' The words came out with a rush.

'You're mad, Sean Mullen. Why would I want to? Doubtless you ask every woman you meet,' she accused, but her heart was thumping. No one had ever asked to be her sweetheart before.

'I'm asking you, aren't I? And I know you want to walk out with me. I can see it in your eyes!' That did it.

'I don't. I'm going to find myself a decent lad, who is not always playing up to every girl he meets. So have your old seal!' She pushed it at him. Then she could see the hard expression return and was sure she had gone too far.

'Mary,' he said, 'you have hurt me.' He wasn't playing; indeed, he looked as though he meant it. There was none of the old joking in his tone.

'I'm sorry,' she said, ' but I only speak where I find. You give me this and say you want to be my sweetheart but,' she shrugged, 'I know nothing about you. And you know nothing of me.'

'That isn't quite true,' he said. 'I know your name and Brala is where you come from. That your Da is dead and that you are coming to America to stay with your Auntie Flynn. That you are seventeen. I know a lot, Mary.'

'But all I know of you is that . . .' she struggled for a moment . . .

'. . . that I am Sean Mullen from Kerry. I am nineteen years old and I intend to make my fortune in the New World. That is all anyone needs to know about my past. It's my future that is important.' Next moment, to Mary's shock, he had his hands around her waist. 'I want to meet you in New York, Mary Flynn. I want your aunt's address, so that I can come calling.'

She could not give away such a secret. It wouldn't be decent. But, inside, something was urging her to tell him, but she ignored the impulse. Her dadda would have smacked her if he'd known what she was thinking. 'I cannot tell you. It wouldn't be right. You are going too far, too fast, Sean Mullen!'

'Then I will give you mine!' he replied passionately and, taking out a penknife, he scratched his name and address on the seal in a fair hand. She stared at it.

'You can read and write?' She looked at him commandingly, arms crossed.

'Did you think I couldn't, Mary Flynn?' he challenged, his eyes flashing. 'Here take back my seal and keep it.' He dropped it into her pocket. She stared down. 'And if you don't want to hear of me again, just throw it into the ocean.' She trembled a little at his passion. 'We dock tomorrow and this is probably the last time we will be talking. But there is one thing I need before we part . . .'

'What?' Mary was confused by the feelings that were tearing through her at the thought she might never see him again.

'To kiss a girl from Ireland!' he breathed and, a moment later, she was in his arms and felt his hot lips on hers. She struggled for a moment, then resigned herself to his embrace, all thoughts of who might be watching, far from her mind.

When he released her, she was dizzy. 'How dare you?' she said weakly and leant against the companionway for support. It had been her very first kiss.

'Because I do!' he said and his eyes were wild. 'Till we meet again, Miss Flynn!' Her lips were still burning as he bowed and was gone as fast as he had come. She hardly knew what she was doing as she stumbled back to her bunk.

Margaret O'Toole caught her by the arm as she began to climb up. 'You are flushed, lady,' she accused. 'Have you let him make free with you?'

'I have not!' Mary said stoutly, defending herself. 'How dare you ask me!'

'Your mother is not here to care for you,' the woman stiffly replied.

'Then I'll take care of myself!' snapped Mary. 'I'm not a child and I'll be pleased if you would keep your nose out of my business.'

'Hoighty-toity!' humphed Mrs O'Toole. 'Ye'll come to a bad end, lady.'

A moment later, Mary was up and into the bed, where she and Bridie cuddled together with her friend begging to know what Sean Mullen had said and done.

'He said nothing, nor did nothing either!' lied Mary to her disappointed friend. Ten minutes later, Bridie was asleep and Mary was taking the seal out of her pocket and hiding it in the bedclothes. Now he'd given it to her, she had no intention of flinging it into the ocean. She never knew when she might need it!

Weeks later, Mary was very glad she had not done so, as she took out the pen and began to write to Sean Mullen, c/o the Shamrock Tree.

She was direct in her request, although ashamed at having to tell him that she had been let down.

My aunt, Margaret Flynn, who you said you wished to meet, has been prevented coming to fetch me after all . . . the letter began, continuing, *I have no desire to return to Ireland and wish to make my home in New York, I would be grateful if you could send me the address of some respectable woman, who would be willing to give me lodgings with her . . .*

However, she did not want Sean to get the idea that she would be in his debt.

If you could kindly arrange the same I assure that when I gain a position in service, I will be most willing to recompense you for your trouble . . . Yours faithfully, Mary Flynn.

She scanned the letter carefully in case she had put something in to it that might compromise her position but came to the conclusion that what she had written was clear. She was asking nothing personally of Sean Mullen.

When the letter was finally finished, Mary was feeling both apprehension and excitement as she folded it in quarters and put it aside ready to give it to Mr McLeish, who collected the post.

When the old Scotsman took it from her hand, he studied the address and regarded her sternly. 'And what are ye thinkin' of writing to a public house, my girl? Who's this young fellow?'

'He's a friend of my family's, who came over on the boat with me, Mr McLeish,' lied Mary. She was not given to telling falsehoods, but desperate times required desperate measures.

'Sean Mullen?' persisted McLeish, wrinkling his forehead as though he was trying to remember the name. Mary prayed that neither would he recall the name, nor ask her any more questions. She was lucky! McLeish had not dealt with the rascal from Kerry.

'Sean's a nice, quiet lad. That's what Mother says anyway.' The mention of her

23

mother seemed to satisfy the man.

'Well, let's hope he moves to a quieter place when he's settled,' McLeish warned. 'The Shamrock Tree is well-known for taking a certain kind of lad, the kind of which you, young lady, should know nothing about. Still, let's hope you get a reply very soon.'

Mary swallowed, thanking God that she had not been found out. The Shamrock Tree was a pub then.

'Trust you, Sean Mullen, to get mixed up with some queer ones,' she muttered under her breath as her feet flew away from McLeish and down the corridor to the peace of her bunk, where she sat for a few moments, her cheeks flaming at the thought of the sin she had committed and what might have happened to her had her father been alive and found out what she'd just done!

CHAPTER THREE

Several dreary weeks dragged by, making Mary think that her letter had never arrived. She was feeling far too melancholy one lovely summer morning, when the sea birds were wheeling in the sky and doing what she wanted to most of all—sweeping over the dull, brown mass of Ellis Island and across the water to land in the sprawling city of New York.

24

If only I could fly, she thought, gazing out of the window so much that several times she pricked herself with her needle, drawing blood. New women and girls had taken the place of Bridie and Mrs O'Toole and, although she had received a letter from the former, scrawled by Bridie's cousin, Pat, wishing Mary good luck, the message had not made her feel any better at all. In fact, it had only made her envious that she was still stuck in the same old place with no hopes of escape.

She was also becoming extremely resentful that she'd had no word yet from Sean Mullen. Maybe he was really bad?

He's a romancer, she told herself firmly, when she was depressed, and a braggart like Mrs O'Toole said. But thinking ill of him made her feel even more miserable, as she couldn't quite believe that, if he'd received her letter, he had left her completely in the lurch.

That sunny morning as she stabbed her needle in and out of the seam of the sheet savagely, it was as if she was stabbing Sean in the heart. Then a hand touched her arm, making her jump.

'You've a visitor!' said Mr McLeish. His expression was wry.

'A visitor?' she repeated, putting down the sheet she was hemming and sucking one of her sore fingers. 'Who is it?' Could it be Sean?

'Come on, girl.' She could see he wasn't letting anything slip. But that was McLeish's

25

way. He took everything soberly. Mary smoothed down her dress as she followed him, conscious of the curious eyes of the girls around her. She didn't care about them or what they thought. It was her turn to get away.

'Is it my aunt?' she asked the Scotsman, running to catch up with him.

'I dinna think so,' was the dry reply, 'but the young woman says that she is your cousin.' He stopped for a moment. 'D'ye have a cousin, Mary Flynn.'

'Indeed, I do, Mr McLeish,' lied Mary. 'And I knew she would come in the end.' But Mary's heart was thumping wildly. Who was this cousin? Her father's sister had no children and she had no other relations in America.

'Ah, weel,' said the old man. 'I'm glad for you, girl. You've had your punishment.'

The girl was not much older than Mary and was dressed fairly well. She had paid a shilling or two for her straw hat, which was trimmed with flowers in the brim. Her hair was a concoction of blonde curls, which might adorn a lady's head but, in this girl's case it was tumbling a little too freely under the hat. Her navy blue dress was of good stuff, but Mary's keen eyes could see that it had been darned in places and not too well either.

She was too finely dressed for a servant, but not well enough for a lady. In fact, the whole of her was a puzzle. As soon as she saw Mary, she ran forward and embraced her, like a lost relative.

'Dear Mary Flynn,' she said, 'my mother has been gravely ill and could not come to meet you.' Mary caught the quizzical look in Mr McLeish's eye and ignored it. 'So she sent for me,' added the young woman, turning to the old Scotsman. 'I am her only daughter, sir, and was in service out of the city. She was too weak to send for me before but, immediately, she recovered, she wrote me a letter and, as soon as my employers would give me leave, I came to fetch Mary. Dear cousin, my mother has told me so much about you, although we have never met. I was so sorry to hear about Uncle dying, although it is good your mother has re-married.'

Mary was too stunned to speak. Perhaps her father had never told her that Aunt Flynn had a daughter? Perhaps it was true? Otherwise how could she know these things? Where had she got her information? Of course, hadn't Mary herself told Sean Mullen . . . She couldn't remember what exactly she'd said to him! 'Come now, kiss your cousin Katy,' cried the girl, who was almost weeping. If she was not Mary's cousin, then she was a very good actress.

'I shall,' replied Mary, throwing caution aside and embracing her. Whoever this girl was, she was the means of her escape. 'I'm so pleased to see you, Katy. How is Auntie Flynn at present?'

'She is much better now she can eat,' said the girl. 'I brought her some comfort with several jars of cow's heel jelly from up country. My mistress is a fair hand at making the stuff, although I do not care for it myself.'

'Have you any identification, Miss?' asked McLeish. 'We cannot let Mary Flynn go from here, unless you can prove your background.' The girl was already rummaging in her bag and produced a large envelope.

'Here is my birth certificate,' she said, 'and papers to prove my identity.' Mr McLeish took them from her hand and scrutinised them.

'They appear to be all in order, but I have to present them to another authority. You must wait here until they are verified.'

'Certainly,' replied the girl. 'In the meantime, Mary, let's go along to your dormitory and start packing.'

With Mr McLeish still staring at the documents, the girls took themselves off through the door and hurried down the corridor. Once they reached where Mary slept, the girl plumped herself down on the bed. Mary looked round to see if anyone was listening. But the place was empty owing to the fact that all the women were on sewing detail.

'Are you really my cousin?' she whispered.

'No, you little goose, of course I'm not, but don't ask me any more questions or you'll never get out of here, and I mean never!'

'But, how . . . ?'

'Don't ask any more questions until we're on the boat,' hissed the girl. 'All you need to know is that I'm Katy Flynn.'

'That's your real name?'

'It is. There are more Flynns in New York than bags of potatoes.'

'Did Sean Mullen send you?' Mary asked breathlessly.

'I said, no more questions, didn't I? D'ye want me to up and leave?'

'Please don't,' Mary begged.

'Then get your things together,' retorted the girl. So Mary packed as fast as she could, feeling her companion's eyes boring into her back when it was turned. Although she had been told not to ask any questions, she found herself dying to know who the girl was.

Was she walking out with Sean Mullen? It was the most uncomfortable thought Mary had harboured since she had thought about what her father would have said had he known she had written familiarly to a strange man.

Even worse, what would he have said now if he had realised that his daughter was about to go off to one of the wickedest cities in the world with a female stranger, who was passing herself off as Mary's cousin for some reason?

However, suddenly Mary realised that she didn't really care as long as she escaped. Dadda was long gone and, sooner or later, if no one came to fetch her, she would be sent back to Ireland. Which would be a terrible fate, given she hated her mother's new husband so much.

No, whoever this Katy Flynn was, Mary had to go along with the subterfuge. New courage entered her breast. This girl was only about her age and could play a part admirably. Well, so could Mary.

'Are ye ready?' asked Katy Flynn, curling her lip disdainfully when she saw Mary's bundles. 'I suppose I'll have to help ye carry them.'

'I can carry them myself,' replied Mary, 'but if you have a mind to help me, I'll be very grateful.'

'How grateful?' asked the girl with interest.

'This grateful?' Pulling out her little drawstring bag, Mary offered a coin.

'Suits me,' replied Katy, taking up the lightest bundle. 'Well, let's take ourselves back to Old Whiskers' office and see if I've been verified.' She must have caught the look of alarm on Mary's face. 'Don't worry. It'll be okay. I've done this before, you know.'

Mary didn't know, but her stomach turned over at the thought. Where was Katy Flynn going to take her and did Sean Mullen know anything about the matter at all?

CHAPTER FOUR

Mary felt sick, not from the horrible moment before Mr McLeish pronounced Katy's documents sound, nor from the boat ride to the shore, but from excitement and apprehension.

She had never been in a city before. She had only been used to the country, green fields and a peaceful village. Indeed, her first taste of raw humanity had come on the voyage on the ship that had carried her to America, which had not been quiet, but it was nothing to the great hustle and bustle of the crowded city of New York.

Mary's eyes darted around, trying to take in the swelling waves of people, who hurried criss-cross in front, each side and behind her, like eager house ants hurrying on their way to their various destinations. Suddenly she felt completely insignificant—the tiniest one of all! And she had never seen the like of the carriages and cabs. She and her companion had already risked their lives three or four times crossing the busy streets.

Mary's ears seemed dulled and hollow with the great noises that assailed them; the sound of traffic and voices rolled into one. All she heard was one mighty echo, that enveloped her as the city rushed into her head.

She gasped and caught her breath, slowing up as she did so—and almost lost Katy Flynn. In a moment, the girl disappeared and, for a minute, Mary panicked. What would she do, all alone in this monstrous place? She knew no one, and had nowhere to go.

A moment later, she felt an impatient tug on her arm. 'What are you doing, you stupid thing? Come on before you get swallowed up in the crowd!'

'I couldn't help it,' replied Mary indignantly. 'I had to stop I had a stitch in my side from hurrying.'

'Oh, stop wingeing,' retorted Katy unkindly and Mary's hackles rose. She'd had almost enough of the girl's impertinence and high-handed ways. Mary's temper was rising.

'I'm not wingeing!' she shouted back determinedly. 'And if you speak to me again like that, Katy Flynn, I'll knock off your hat!'

'I'd like to see that!' Katy faced her, but there was less of a sneer in her voice. 'Ah, come on, Mary. I was only kidding you. We're nearly there anyway.'

It was then Mary realised that she was going to have to stick up for herself in New York. These were tough people and she would have no one else but her own sharp tongue and fists as defence.

Finally, they entered into a maze of dark alleyways, that frightened Mary. Was she destined to be murdered? Strange old fellows tottered by, many the worse for drink and dirty, little urchins played in the gutter, with no one to watch them. This was not what she had come to America for—she had come seeking a better life!

'I don't like this place,' she said.

'Sure, neither do I,' replied Katy. Mary looked at her with surprise. The girl added, 'It wouldn't do to be walking around here late, I can tell you, but it's a short cut.'

Two minutes later, they were standing in an open square, surrounded by what seemed to be the tallest houses Mary had ever seen. Her eyes must have shown her surprise. Katy said, 'These are called tenements, Mary Flynn. Most of us live here until we can do better.'

Mary frowned but, a moment later, she was drawing in her breath. Straight in front of her swung an inn sign, emblazoned with a great three-leaved plant she knew well. A plant as big as a tree!

'Ay,' said Katy dryly. 'The Shamrock Tree is very well-known in this neighbourhood.'

A moment later, they were walking past it and their ears were assaulted with piercing whistles from several men, who leaned out several of the upstairs windows and shouted at them rudely, 'Come you in, Katy Flynn. And bring in your pretty companion!'

Mary's face grew bright red. She was not used to such people. No man in her village would ever have behaved so. It was then she thought of Sean Mullen. How come he would live in such a place? Her cheeks blazed as Katy yelled in a manner unfit for any woman,

'Get away with you, Mick. Go back to your pots, you villains!' She looked at Mary and grinned, 'See what I mean. Working men have little manners.'

'Yes,' said Mary, hoping that where she was going did not harbour any such fellows. Soon the two girls were walking down a narrow entry, through a door and facing a tall flight of wooden steps. It was already getting dark and Mary felt exhausted with the day's happenings.

'Take a breath now, Mary,' said Katy. 'This is the first flight—only ten to go.'

'Ten,' gasped Mary as she began to climb. Soon her bundles felt like lead and her brains seemed to be bursting from her head. 'I have to stop,' she gasped. Katy was puffing too.

'Good thing we don't have to do twenty. Although I have run up five!' The girl's eyes twinkled at Mary's discomfiture.

Mary breathed in deeply. For one moment, she wished she was back in Ireland. But that soon passed off, as she lugged her baggage up the never-ending flights of stairs. At least, she was in America itself and off Ellis Island. And, soon, she might see Sean.

Finally, the girls stood panting in front of a substantial-looking door, which was losing all its paint, where it appeared to have been kicked by heavy boots.

A stab of fear ran through Mary, but she tried to control her breathing and her apprehension, as Katy gave a sharp knock.

'Who's there?' The voice was a woman's and Irish.

'Katy Flynn.' Next moment, Mary heard the bolt being drawn back and found herself face to face with a middle-aged woman of large stature. It must be Katy's Ma, thought Mary. But the woman was not smiling.

'Well, don't just stand there. Come in, the two of you. And wipe your feet!' Her voice was rough. Mary followed Katy into a room, the like of which she had never seen before.

It seemed to be large and full of curtains, not at the window only, which was large and high, but festooned about the room. Old, grey muslins and faded, worn, red velvets hung down to the floor, partitioning off a portion here and there.

Is it a shop, Mary thought? Maybe she's the shopkeeper? Several easy chairs were scattered about the room. Once they had been fine specimens, similar to those that Mary had seen in the gentleman's house back in Ireland, but these chairs had faded upholstery and some of the stuffing was hanging out from beneath the seats.

A large oval mirror, which once had glittered, reflected the scene from where it hung over a black-leaded fireplace, in which a fire burned dully. A large, brown teapot sat on

35

the hob, opposite a kettle with steam coming out of the spout.

Then Mary's eyes met the woman's, who was looking her over without speaking, making Mary feel very uncomfortable. She wore the same shabby finery that Katy did. In addition and incongruously, she had two feathers stuck in the back of her piled-up red hair. Her over-dress was made of what had once been fine silk stuff, but like Katy's had been mended over and over again. However, she was clean and Mary caught a whiff of very strong scent.

'So this is the Mary Flynn we have been hearing about,' declared the woman, putting her hands on her hips. Mary was puzzled.

'Yes, I'm Mary Flynn. But what have you heard about me? I don't know you.'

'I have heard a lot about you, girl,' said the woman, grinning to reveal several bad, front teeth. 'I am Maggie Teal and I don't like girls who ask too many questions. And as for you, miss, you have done your work, now be off with you and earn your living!'

All this time, Katy had been standing without saying a word. She looked about to remonstrate, but seemed suddenly to change her mind and obeyed like a sheep does before a dog. A moment later, the door was closing behind her and Mary was left alone with Maggie Teal.

'Who are you?' asked Mary. 'Do you know Sean Mullen?'

'You ask a lot of questions for a poor immigrant just off Ellis Island,' replied the woman and Mary felt a warning in her tone.

'I only ask what I am due,' replied Mary.

'Sassy!' exclaimed the woman.

'I don't understand you,' persisted Mary. 'Why won't you answer my questions? Who are you? Do you know Sean?'

'Oh, aye, I know him, together with the rest of this part of New York,' said the woman dryly.

Mary's heart leaped. Then he had sent for her. But why hadn't he come himself? Of course, it must have been because Mr McLeish might have recognised him.

'What are you thinking, girl, that lights up your eyes like a flame? Are you carrying a torch for the young fella?'

'I am not,' said Mary spiritedly. 'Nothing improper has ever taken place between us!'

'Well, that's a relief. Sit yourself down.' The woman's eyes twinkled and Mary was sure that she was making fun of her, but she obeyed as she felt extremely tired after the day's excitement as well as lugging her belongings up ten flights of stairs.

A moment later, Maggie disappeared behind one of the hanging drapes and Mary heard the rattle of cups. She lay back against the chair and closed her eyes. It seemed only a second later that the woman was handing her a cup, full of what appeared to be strong tea.

'Drink this. It will make you feel better. You've a pale face on you, Mary Flynn, and you will be good-for-nothing if you don't rest.'

'What is it?' asked Mary suspiciously.

'Strong, old tea with a dash of whisky in it. It'll do you good.'

'I don't drink,' said Mary.

'Drink it,' ordered Maggie. 'It will do you no harm.'

'Thank you.' Mary sipped it slowly. It did taste comfortingly good. So many questions were going through her head, but her brain seemed dizzy. She finished the tea, while the woman watched her every move.

'Now—get you behind here. You look like you need to sleep. You'll feel better in the morning.' Maggie beckoned Mary to follow her behind another set of drapes, covering a grubby door. Mary rose and, a moment later, was entering a crude sort of bedroom, which had only a narrow bed and a dresser. Not even a window to see out of. But the bed was clean and already turned down invitingly. 'Sit down!' ordered Maggie and a tired Mary obeyed and collapsed on what was a very old but comfortable feathered eiderdown.

'My things,' she said, anxiously looking across towards the door.

'I'll bring them in for you. Put on the night dress over there.' Mary stared in its direction. It was white and ruffled. 'It's clean. Then lie down and get some rest. Don't look so scared.

38

You are quite safe here.'

Mary had little option to do what Maggie said. Besides, she was too tired to do anything else as the whisky had gone right to her head.

CHAPTER FIVE

Mary woke drowsily and could not think where she was. She must have been very tired indeed. But the dim light in the unfamiliar room told her it was morning.

Then she remembered that she was in a strange woman's house and she had been there all night. She was about to jump up, but sank back into the pillow as she heard voices in the next room. The noise must have been what had woken her. Her head ached miserably. That must have been the whisky.

Suddenly, she heard her name. They were talking about her! Lifting her head, she listened keenly to what they were saying, but she couldn't make it all out. Her mother had always reminded her, 'Nothing good ever comes of eavesdropping!' And, in this case, it didn't.

'What are we going to do with the girl? I can't keep her for nothing!' That was the woman, whom Mary had supposed to be Katy's ma, but had turned out to be called Maggie Teal. Her voice was raised and shrill.

'Well, we can't do what we would usually do, woman, can we?' replied the man in a hard voice. 'Not with Sean around.'

Mary's heart gave a jump. Not only on account of the fact the speaker had mentioned Sean, but that, for a moment, she had been reminded of her stepfather's voice, back in Ireland. That was how he had spoken to her mother sometimes. Cruelly, especially when he was in a bad temper.

And what did they mean 'what were they going to do with her'? Mary panicked momentarily, thinking that she must fly out and ask them what they meant. But some scrap of sense mercifully prevented her.

'Is she in there?' asked the man.

'She is—and you can't go in!' replied Maggie. Mary closed her eyes and stiffened her body. If he did, she'd be asleep. But he did not.

Mary swallowed and opened her eyes again, looking around for some means of escape, but there was none. Not even a little window! Besides, she was ten floors up. She couldn't hear what the couple were saying any more and she didn't care. All she wanted to do was get away and find Sean. He would protect her, she was sure of that.

He might have behaved in an improper way to her, seeing her without a chaperone, but he had been the only man who had ever said that he wanted to be her sweetheart. That he wanted to walk out with her. That he would come calling on her Aunt Flynn.

Then her eyes filled with tears. Mary was not given easily to crying. She had seen too much sadness. But she couldn't stop. Why hadn't Auntie come for her? She must be dead and, now, Mary was all alone in America.

Suddenly, Mary remembered Mrs O'Toole's warnings about Sean. She had called him a devil. Was he? Mary was about to sink into despair, when she realised that self-pity was doing her no good. She had to be strong and she had to find out why she had been brought to this place. She also had to discover how Sean was involved with these people.

Making sure that the voices had ceased and, sure after hearing the door slam, she made a show of yawning, stretching and going over to the drapes and peeping through shyly.

Maggie Teal was sifting in her chair, pouring herself some strong brew from the brown teapot. She looked even more blowsy in daylight. She had feathers in her hair no longer, but was wearing a long nightdress trimmed with torn lace, covered over with a dressing-gown of some material, which in the past, might have been satin, but was now very old and scraggy.

Immediately, it struck Mary that she had been entertaining a man in her night clothes! Maybe it was her husband?

'Ah, you're up,' she sniffed, smiling weakly.

41

'Do you want some tea?'

'I will, thank you,' said Mary, thinking she must do something to escape, whatever happened. It was now or never! She took the cup with a prim smile and sipped daintily from it, like a lady does.

'You have good manners, I see,' replied Maggie in an interested way. 'Doubtless you come of a good family.'

'I hope I do,' said Mary. 'And that is why I would like you to help me find my Auntie Flynn, Mrs Teal.' She was going to butter up the woman or she might never get out of the place.

'Your Auntie Flynn?' Maggie seemed genuinely surprised. 'You have other relatives in New York then?' That other must mean Maggie believed that she was related to Sean.

'I have—and they are business people,' said Mary. It was only half a lie.

'So—you and Sean Mullen came over together?' asked Maggie, seeming even more interested.

'We did,' Mary added, knowing that whatever Sean was up to, she must play along with it as her only means of escape.

'Sean promised that, if Aunt Flynn didn't come to fetch me, he would do his best to find out if she was well and, if so, would take me to her himself. Doubtless, she has been too busy to come and find me.' Mary could see that Sean Mullen was definitely somebody that counted. She remembered suddenly that he said he was descended from high folk.

'With the business?' asked Maggie. Mary nodded in reply.

'What business was that, then?' Maggie was a bit too curious. At least, on this fact, Mary had no need to lie.

'My aunt keeps a small hotel ...'

'A hotel, is it?' That had certainly startled Maggie.

'And she was expecting me to help her to run it. The business side, I mean. I am good at things like that, having had an education.' That was true too.

Maggie didn't answer for a moment, then asked, 'Where was this establishment?' Mary knew the address off by heart, but did not give it fully. She was far too astute. She only gave the name of the street.

'Oh, dear,' said Maggie. 'Oh, dear, dear me.'

'What's the matter?' Mary hoped her voice was not shaking.

'That part of the town was burned down only in February. It was a mighty conflagration. There was a deal of boarding-houses over there and a great loss of life.' Mary hardly noticed the slight mockery as she was feeling numb at such terrible news. 'Child, I fear that your auntie is dead and buried.'

To Mary's horror, her lip began to tremble and a large tear rolled down her cheek. Maggie added, 'Come on now, girlie, don't cry.

Your aunt's soul is in Heaven, if she is the good woman I am sure she was.'

'I can't be thinking she's dead,' replied Mary with a sob in her voice. 'Sean would have told me.'

'And that he will, my poor, little bird,' soothed Maggie Teal, 'but, maybe, he doesn't know yet. Now, drink up your tea and try not to think about it.' She filled up Mary's half-drunk cup with the dark, brown liquid, then put the pot down slowly. 'Maybe there will be some money to come to you from your aunt?'

'Maybe,' said Mary, but all she could think of was her Auntie Flynn perishing screaming amidst the flames and, nearly as bad, Mary's only hope of a decent escape gone for ever.

Suddenly, she was wondering how on earth she was going to carry on making conversation. She had nothing at all in common with this woman, and she needed to find Sean. 'I should get dressed now,' she added sombrely.

'Not in those old things you can't,' said Maggie.

'Do you mean my clothes?' asked Mary offended. 'Have you been looking in my bags. How dare you?'

'Sassy!' replied Maggie. 'I happened to peep inside when I was moving them. You're a pretty girl and you should be fitted up as such. You're in New York now, you know.'

'You think we were all old-fashioned in Ireland?' Mary's mettle was up.

44

'Cool down, miss. I'm not saying anything about the old country, God love it. But in America we must be smarter and new. I have just the thing to suit you.' At that, Maggie dragged herself out of her chair and disappeared behind another set of drapes.

Mary could feel her face going red at the insult she had just taken. She knew that her clothes were a little worn, but she had some decent, new ones in the bag, which she had been saving for meeting her Auntie Flynn. She hadn't worn them to come here with Katy in case they were spoiled. And now this rude woman was making sport of them.

'I don't care to see any new clothes,' she called. There was no reply from the invisible room. Mary frowned, but a moment later, her eyes opened wide as Maggie emerged with a dress laid over her arm. It was a gown the kind of which Mary had only seen on very fine ladies. She caught her breath.

'Ah, you like this one then. So will he.' Maggie's sly grin incensed Mary.

'To whom are you referring?'

'Why Sean Mullen, of course. He likes his young ladies . . .' Maggie had evidently changed her mind about finishing the sentence which, although Mary understood perfectly, did not want to hear.

'He was civil enough when I wore my old plaid,' Mary's words were sharp.

'And why shouldn't he be, you being such a

good-looking young woman,' sniffed Maggie. 'Now, this will match those eyes of yours.' The gown was a magnificent blue. Mary had not imagined her eyes were of that hue, but she resisted answering sharply. Her heart had leaped at the sight of the finery.

'I cannot afford to pay for this,' she said bluntly. 'At least, not until I have heard about Auntie Flynn.' Mary crossed herself quickly.

'You do not have to pay for it. It was bought for another young lady, who stayed here some time and, sadly, now is gone.' Mary shivered inside. What had happened to that girl?

'I can't take it,' she replied.

'Come on now,' wheedled the woman. 'You want Sean to see you looking well. He is a fine, young man himself these days. Dressed to the nines!'

'Does he come here often?' probed Mary. Somehow, she could not see Sean in this strange environment. She had a flash of when she had first caught sight of him, the wind making his shirt fly wildly off his hard-muscled body.

'Sure you are blushing,' pointed out Maggie slyly. 'Indeed, he does not come here much. He has other fish to fry.' She laid the dress over Mary's arm. It felt heavenly against the bare skin of her wrist.

'What fish? Is he in business?'

'That he is,' Maggie laughed. Mary had an angry suspicion she was laughing at her again.

'Now slip on the gown. I know you want to. In any case, I would like to see you in it. It would not suit our Katy.'

'Doesn't Katy sleep here?' asked Mary. 'I hope I didn't take her place.'

'Indeed you did not. She stayed with a friend last night. Now slip on the dress, please.' Mary was beginning to relent. It was so beautiful and there seemed no harm in it. It was such a long time since she'd worn anything nice.

'All right,' she said. Maggie clapped her hands.

'There's a very pretty hat to go with it. You may have that too.'

'I would like to wash first,' said Mary. The idea of being dressed up was suddenly quite frightening.

'Just go in there.' Maggie indicated the same partition from which she'd brought the dress. 'There's a pan boiling in the kitchen. I'll bring water for you.'

'Thank you,' replied Mary, walking across and pulling aside the dusty drapes. She gasped. It was a real dressing room. One of the large cupboard doors was slightly open and Mary peeped inside curiously.

It must be a shop, she thought. The cupboard was full of dresses. What was Maggie Teal doing with all those? The way she dressed, she couldn't possibly be the owner of such finery. Suddenly, Mary felt she shouldn't be looking and quickly withdrew. The rest of the room's furniture was a larger bed than the one she had slept in, a full-length mirror, a chest of drawers and a dark washstand with a great white porcelain jug and bowl.

A few minutes later, that bowl was full of heavenly warm water and Mary was soaping herself with a fragrant rose-scented block. She felt a new girl—almost. But when she dressed herself in the blue gown, she was completely transformed.

She rarely stared at herself in the mirror as she was not vain, but when she did she could hardly believe she was Mary Flynn, recently come off Ellis Island.

'You look beautiful,' cooed Maggie Teal. Mary swung around embarrassed. 'The colour suits you as I thought it would.'

Why did this woman want to dress her up for Sean?

Maggie Teal was bending to open a drawer at the bottom of one of the cupboards. 'Let's top the outfit with this,' she said, pulling out one of the loveliest hats Mary had ever seen. It matched the dress exactly.

'I can't accept it,' she replied. Where was all the dressing up leading?

'I'm not giving it to you, girlie. It's on loan.'

'Why?' asked Mary stubbornly. She had learned enough on the ship to know that no one did anything for nothing.

'I told you. Sean Mullen is an important

man hereabouts and you can't go visiting him looking like a pauper.' Maggie had a crafty look in her eyes, that Mary didn't particularly like. Suddenly Mary thought she understood. Maggie Teal wanted to make an impression on Sean and she was using Mary to do it.

'Thank you,' she replied primly. 'I will be pleased to wear the gown.'

'Certainly, miss,' said Maggie. 'Now come on and take some breakfast. You will need something inside you before you go to The Shamrock Tree.'

Mary started with alarm. Was that where she was to meet Sean? That place where those rude men had called and whistled after the two girls. She had fancied that Sean and herself would be meeting in some pretty tea room.

'What's up, my fine lady?' asked Maggie.

'I'm not sure that my mother would like me entering a public house,' she replied. Maggie laughed out loud. Mary frowned. 'I don't like being made fun of,' she added. 'Besides, I think the place may not have a good reputation.'

'You wrote to it, but you would not enter?'

'How did you know I wrote there?' asked Mary.

'I have read your letter,' replied Maggie. Mary could hardly believe that Sean had shown her letter all over the town. Maggie must be given to lying. If she had really read Mary's letter, then she would have known about her Aunt Flynn. Mary drew her eyebrows together in a frown. Why should she believe Maggie? Maybe she was misjudging Sean? On the other hand, Mary had asked Sean to find her lodgings with some respectable woman.

'Don't worry,' added the woman. 'I was asked to fetch you by a good friend of the man himself. And was ordered that no harm would come to you. The public bar is not for ladies, but there are several private rooms a young lady may enter unobserved.' Her eyes twinkled.

'And it's there you are bound. Don't worry, Miss Flynn, your honour will not be compromised. Now come through to your breakfast. You'll need a napkin for fear you spoil your gown. Better hurry up. That Katy Flynn will be here directly to take you to The Shamrock.' With that, she pulled the curtains back and beckoned Mary into the living space.

Mary's head was in a whirl. Who was this friend of Sean's? Could it be the man she had overheard talking to Maggie? But he sounded so unpleasant and frightening! Yet, maybe this was the way people behaved in the city. Maybe it was not shameful to be seen in a public house with a man? One thing she knew, she wanted to see Sean Mullen again more than anything else in the world.

CHAPTER SIX

Katy arrived to fetch Mary a few minutes after eleven. 'And where do you think you've been, miss? Keeping me waiting!' scolded Maggie Teal. Mary felt extremely embarrassed, especially since she was dressed so finely and her would-be companion was not. Strangely enough, the fiery Katy did not remonstrate against the telling-off. She only fidgeted and twisted the string handle of the bag she was carrying as if she didn't want to let go of it.

'Come with me, you,' Maggie ordered. Katy walked across the room. It was as if Maggie had a hold over the girl, even though she was not her Ma. Mary was surprised at the change in Katy's demeanour, given her earlier feisty behaviour.

Mary stood uncertainly, then made to follow, but Maggie turned to her sharply and said, 'Stay there, miss. This girl and I have business.' Then Maggie took Katy into the bedroom and drew the drapes behind them. Evidently, they had a secret!

Mary would have dearly loved to know what they were saying to one another. However, her experience of eavesdropping on Maggie and her male visitor earlier that morning had put her off!

When the two eventually emerged, Katy

51

appeared more sullen than ever and regarded Mary with what she recognised as some jealousy. Indeed, Katy looked her over from top to toe with hard, bright eyes and never said a word.

Mary fancied she must have been told off about her appearance as well as her lateness. Indeed, Katy looked as if she'd had an exceedingly rough night all together and she was no longer clutching the small, string bag she'd been carrying when she came in.

'Are you ready then?' muttered Katy.

'She's ready,' replied Maggie, 'and a beautiful sight she is too!'

'Oh ay,' agreed Katy with a bad grace and Mary knew instinctively that the girl envied her deeply. Which was quite a shock. In fact, everything that had happened since she had spent the night with Maggie Teal had become a puzzle. What was going on in this strange house with its even stranger visitors?

'See you later, Miss Flynn,' Maggie called, but Mary saw her eyes were mocking.

'Will my baggage be safe?' asked Mary. 'Or shall I take it with me?'

'What? In that outfit?' laughed both Maggie and Katy. Mary could see they were right, but she was still uneasy leaving all she owned with them. But she had seen fit to keep the small amount of money she had on her person ever since she had left Ellis Island. Biting her lip, she followed Katy out of the room.

As Mary and Katy turned out of the narrow alleyway and into the broad city street, her eyes were dazzled by not only the day's brightness, but by the press of people, hurrying about like swarms of crazy insects.

The noise they made came in waves, crashing through her unaccustomed ears. The shouts and cries of tradesmen, the wheels of carts, the trotting of horses and every noise a great city is full of, and which can hardly be understood by a country dweller, made Mary light-headed as her unaccustomed eyes drank them all in, lifting her earlier mood into a rush of awe and excitement.

However she had felt earlier, she could hardly think of anything now, except that in a few minutes she would be meeting Sean again. She wondered if he had changed since he had courted her on the ship. She was so wrapped up in her own thoughts that she almost stepped in front of a cab.

'Watch yourself!' shouted Katy, dragging her backwards.

'Sorry!' cried Mary, trying to compose herself.

'You will be, if you don't stop gawping!' shouted Katy unkindly over the noise of the traffic, 'and lift your skirts higher. You don't want to get that dress filthy.'

They picked their way back the route they had come the night before and across another busy street until, finally, Mary found herself

53

standing on the pavement outside The Shamrock Tree.

At that moment, she wished she had never written that bold letter to Sean Mullen. She could feel herself shaking from nerves, mixed with reckless excitement. She wondered if he was changed. She certainly looked different.

'Come on then, Mary Flynn,' called Katy as she lifted the knocker and banged on the door. 'Let's wake those lads out of their drunken sleep!'

Mary swallowed nervously, pausing breathlessly beside her companion outside the heavy, iron-bound door, but still trying to look nonchalant and experienced. Yet she was unable to resist an upwards glance towards the windows from where those rude, young fellows had shouted at Katy the night before. Now the window panes were black and the curtains closed.

Well, whether it was a decent place or not, she was about to find out for herself. And whether Sean himself was a decent lad was an idea that turned Mary's stomach right over. A moment later, the door was opened by a bedraggled, red-haired boy in a cap, who looked about twelve. 'Come on in, misses, if you please,' he said, but mischief darted in his eyes.

'Who do you think you are, calling us "misses"?' snapped Katy. 'Get back to your stool! We have an appointment with Mr

Michael Mallon.' The boy made a face and, closing the door, sat down again. Once more, Mary wondered what business the man had with her and why she would not be meeting Sean straight away. But she was here now and her questions would soon be answered . . .

Breathing in deeply to give her courage, she lifted up her blue gown daintily, bravely stepped over the step and walked through the door into the cobbled courtyard of the public house, enclosed all round by stark, tenement buildings.

There was no warmth in this place. The cold wind swept across the courtyard making Mary shiver as though it was winter not spring.

A huddle of old tarred barrels were hustled into a corner and scraps of rubbish were being blown about aimlessly, while in one corner were the remains of several smashed glasses. And not a sign of life!

Suddenly, she found herself longing for the country and green fields. But she knew she would see none in this city.

'Stop mooning about!' ordered Katy, nastily.

'Is there no one here? It's all so quiet.' How Mary wished she had a friend to confide in. Bridie, for instance.

'It wasn't last night,' snapped Katy. For the first time that morning she smiled, but it was an unpleasant grin. Mary wanted to ask her what she had been doing in a public house at night, but changed her mind.

Her spirits sank even more as they crossed the courtyard and began to climb an outside flight of iron stairs to a worn door. Mary was ready to run.

'We're here,' Katy called in a loud voice. A dog's great bark came from the inside and, a moment later, a rough-looking fellow in a cap opened the door and, grinning, touched his headgear.

Was this the man they were to meet, thought Mary? But Katy passed by him without a word. At the end of a corridor, which smelled of ale, a big shaggy dog stood, ears erect . . .

Mary heard its low growl and shivered. 'Come off,' a man's voice barked and the dog turned obediently and went into a room with Katy in tail. Mary couldn't believe it when she followed. It was quite different from anything she had imagined. The room was a gentleman's. Fine furniture and elegant drapes.

'Come in, young ladies. Will you take a drink?' A tall, well-dressed man had his back to them. His hair was as dark as Sean's, but streaked with grey. His clothes were smart like a gentleman's, his suit was made of fine fabric.

'Katy?' he asked, turning two glasses in his hand.

'If you please, Mr Mallon.' Katy rushed forward and grabbed the glass. Mary stood still, struck cold by the voice. When he first turned, she knew she had never seen his face before, but she realised instinctively that this was the voice she had heard earlier on at Maggie Teal's. The visitor who wanted to 'do something with her' but couldn't because of Sean.

Smiling, he was stretching out his hand, which she took, hoping he wouldn't feel her's tremble.

'Lovely, by God,' he murmured. 'You're welcome, Miss Flynn.'

'Mr Mallon,' she replied, her voice clear and high.

'Will you take a drink too?' he asked, offering her the other glass.

'I will not,' she said. 'I have never taken strong drink.'

'Then you should try, Miss Flynn. It's very soothing.'

'I don't think so,' she said coldly, then remembered the tea she had drunk last night and blushed.

'It's good to see roses start in your cheeks. That's not something we're used to here, eh, Katy?'

'To be sure, Mr Mallon.' Katy was deferential.

'Drink up now, girl. I need to be speaking to Miss Mary alone.'

'And I need to see Sean Mullen,' added Mary, almost alarmed at her own boldness and wishing that Katy, however ungracious would

57

stay. But the girl had already sidled to the door and left.

'You have spirit, I see, Miss Mary.' He grinned. 'Sit yourself down, if you please. I have sent for Sean and he'll be here directly.' Mary took the chair indicated and quickly mulled over what he'd just said. Did he employ Sean then?

'How do you know Sean?' she asked.

'Ah, that would be a story.' One, which was quite obvious he was not prepared to tell. He went over and poured himself a glass of whisky. 'We should drink to the old country, but I never make toasts alone,' he said. 'Now I believe you wrote to the lad, asking to come here.'

'I did, but only to ask his help in finding my dear aunt.' Mary's eyes filled with tears involuntarily.

'Of course. I believe she was consumed in the fire?'

'How did you know that?'

'I was speaking to an acquaintance of yours. Mrs Teal.'

'And when was that, Mr Mallon?' probed Mary.

'Why only this morning, to be sure,' he said. 'So, if your poor aunt is gone, then what shall we do with you?' Mary's heart jumped. Was that what he'd meant? Maybe it was all innocence, but her instincts told her not to trust him. Besides, she didn't like the way he looked at her, his eyes roving over her body, like a tinker's at a horse fair.

'I will shift for myself,' replied Mary. 'I am beholden to no one except Mr Mullen, who has been a good friend to me.'

'Sean was a good friend indeed to introduce you to The Shamrock Tree, of which I am the proud proprietor.' Mallon rose from his seat and went over to Mary. 'We've had many a bonny lass come here with requests to find lost relatives.' He leaned over her and she could smell the whisky on his breath. 'And we have been able to help them. Please let me help you, Miss Mary.' She didn't like his tone, nor the look in his eyes.

'No thank you, Mr Mallon. I am sure that Sean will help me find my aunt. She may be still alive.' At least, Mary could still hope.

'I'm sure he will,' he replied, 'but that will all depend on me.' He regarded her steadily, like a snake does its prey.

'Why?' Her voice trembled, thinking that what he said couldn't be true.

'Sean is my employee. And a busy, young man he is too,' added Mallon. 'If you know what is good for you, you will let me aid you. Don't you know who you are talking to?' Mallon was fingering the blue silk of her wrist as if he owned her.

'Stop, please,' she said breathlessly. 'I can see you are no gentleman, sir, to threaten me so. I want to see Sean!'

'Oh, you want your prince to rescue you!' laughed Mallon, but his eyes were cold. 'I am as good as any young one, miss. Young men are often cruel. I think you would be well advised to take up my offer.' He grasped her arm and his strong fingers dug into her flesh.

'I will not,' cried Mary heatedly. To her horror, tears started in her eyes, pricking them like thorns.

'What do you think I am going to do with you, Miss Flynn?' asked Mallon slyly, his breath in her face again.

'I don't know, but whatever you think, you will not!' she retorted, trying to pull away. She felt sick inside, wondering what she had got herself into. She was now standing so close to him that she could hardly breathe.

Suddenly, she heard the door burst open and felt Mallon let her go. Her eyes flicked shut in one second of relief, then she swung round.

'Sean! Sean! Thank goodness, you're here.' She ran to him without thinking, all her former inhibitions forgotten; escaped into his arms as if he was her sweetheart already, as if she'd known him for years.

His surprising response was to kiss her hard on the lips in a very ungentlemanly way that set her heart pounding. She was about to struggle when he relinquished her lips and muttered in her ear, 'Don't move. Trust me!'

She was full of indignation, but she let him

hold her close. 'What's going on, Mallon?' he spat over her shoulder, still holding on to her. Mary, dizzy with anger and feelings inside she could hardly understand, could hear his heart thudding fast as her head and body were pressed against him.

'Very little, Sean,' lied the man. 'I was trying to convince Miss Flynn of my desire to help her. I believe she still thinks she's in Ireland. Customs are different in New York, my dear. We are all Americans now.' Mary still couldn't disengage herself from Sean's arms.

'What happened, Mary?' asked Sean, looking down at her.

'He was making advances towards me,' she replied, her voice trembling.

'Was he indeed?' Sean asked, lifting up her chin, his eyes searching her face. 'Now, calm down. Maybe Mr Mallon was only trying to be friendly.'

She looked at him now, she hardly knew him, he was so fine. His face was finely shaved and he was wearing a better Sunday suit than her father had ever worn. It was navy-blue with slight stripes.

Sean's collar was high and starched. Above it, his hair had grown longer, which was not the fashion, but suited him well. He was entirely a different man from the one she remembered. The coldness in her changed quickly to disappointment, which was then replaced by fear, making her wary. He must

61

have felt her withdraw from him because, a moment later, the warm prison of his arms had disappeared and she was entirely alone.

'I'm sorry,' she said. The two men were regarding her strangely. Mallon's eyes were like a watchful animal's, while Sean's were brooding. 'Perhaps I misunderstood. I'm sorry if I insulted you, sir.'

'And I you. Come, let us all be friends and take a small drink together. Isn't she a fine, young woman, Sean? She dresses up beautifully. You've done well.'

'I don't need your compliments, Mallon. Neither does she.'

'Indeed, you will. Yes, you two young people should have some time to talk. Miss Flynn will find out that we can be hospitable here, will she not, Sean?'

'You will, Mary,' agreed Sean. She was so disappointed. Was this the lad she had depended on? He was just as handsome, but probably as false. How could he have wanted to walk out with her, when he evidently didn't care one jot?

But, then, what did he mean when he'd asked her to trust him? She was completely confused.

They stood in silence, as Mallon strode over to the sideboard and poured out three drinks and carried them over. 'None for me, sir,' Mary remonstrated but he still thrust the glass into her hand.

'Come now,' he said, 'this is a public house and the whisky is free to young ladies I take a fancy to.'

'She said no,' interposed Sean suddenly and his voice was hard and rasping like a file on iron. 'I'll drink it instead.' He took her glass and drained it. Mallon didn't argue, only took a slug from his own.

'Still playing the gentleman,' remarked Mallon sarcastically, but his face had gone a trifle pale. Mary, who was still recovering from her surprise at Sean's sudden defence of her, realised that what she'd suspected, after the conversation she'd overheard between Maggie Teal and Mallon, was true. Sean's boss was afraid of him.

The two men faced each other, then Mallon said ungraciously, 'You can take two hours off to get Mary Flynn settled.'

'I'll need more than that,' replied Sean.

'I get your drift,' the other leered and Mary's cheeks flamed. 'Well, then, be sure you're back at your post before closing time.' Sean nodded.

'Farewell, Miss Flynn. Doubtless I'll be seeing your lovely self very soon.' Then Mallon sprawled into the chair and waved them both away.

A moment later, Sean's hand slipped into hers and held it fast. She didn't remonstrate until they were outside the door.

'What do you think you're up to, Sean

Mullen, kissing me like that in front of that man?' she raged.

'Quiet! Come on,' Sean ordered and, a moment later, he was almost dragging her down the stairs and across the courtyard and up another flight.

'I don't want to go up,' said Mary, halting stubbornly.

'Don't be a goose,' Sean snapped. 'Do as I tell you and you'll be all right.' Soon, they were walking swiftly along a corridor and stopped outside a door at the end. Sean took out a key and opened it. 'Go in,' he said. 'Go!' as Mary hesitated. 'I'm not going to hurt you, I promise,' he added.

'All right,' said Mary, and stepped inside. The room was more like home. Like Ireland. A bright fire burned in the grate and a kettle and a teapot stood on the hob. The table had a pitcher on it and two cups were laid. A loaf of soda bread sat on a board together with a bowl of butter. Sean pointed to a comfortable, old chair positioned by the fire.

'Sit down. You look worn out.' As she crossed, she saw a bed positioned behind a half-drawn drape. It was untidy with a man's clothes. 'Yes, this is my room,' said Sean, following her eyes. 'And you have nothing to be afraid of, Mary Flynn.'

'Haven't I?' she asked with a sob.

'You have not,' he said, taking off his jacket and flinging it down. 'Now you'll take some

64

tea, won't you?'

'Yes, if you please,' replied Mary, stifling her tears. She was not used to seeing a man behaving as a housewife, but she liked it. Soon she was seated with tea and a great slab of bread and butter beside her.

'Sorry it's not too dainty,' he said, 'but I do not possess a carving knife. I take my other meals in the pub.' She ate the bread hungrily, while he slid down on the mat in front of the fire and gazed into the flames.

'I have a confession to make,' Sean said suddenly. 'I fear that I told Mallon we were engaged to be married,' replied Sean solemnly. A dark expression crossed his face and she was almost afraid to scold him. But she had to.

'You had no right!' exclaimed Mary. 'It's not decent.'

'Nothing here is decent, Mary. This is New York. It's a rough, old place.'

'What do you mean?' asked Mary. 'When I wrote to you, I asked if you could find my aunt and, if not, a place in service with a decent, God-fearing woman. I didn't ask to be brought here.'

'Mary, I will try and help you to find your aunt, if she's still alive but, before that, I have to protect you. The Shamrock Tree is not a good place.'

'I guessed that,' cried Mary bitterly. 'I have to get out.'

'That will be difficult without my help,' said

Sean. 'That is why I lied about us and have brought you to my room. Otherwise you could be in danger.'

'Danger?' She was tortured by wanting to tell him about the conversation she had overheard, but she wasn't quite sure yet whether she could trust him.

'Aye,' replied Sean.

'What kind of danger?'

'The kind any unprotected, pretty, young woman faces in a great city,' he said. 'Why do you think they kept you so long on Ellis Island?'

'I can look after myself,' she said.

Sean laughed. 'As spirited as ever, Mary Flynn. But too many spirits have been sunk in The Shamrock Tree.'

'Why do you remain here then?' she asked.

'I can't explain.'

'Why was I brought to Maggie Teal's instead of here directly?'

'Because, Mary, you were marked out. Your letter was intercepted and it was only by my lies to Mallon that no harm has come to you. And that is why you have to go along with what I have told them. You have to stay here with me.'

'What? Here?' She looked wildly round the room. How could she?

'Yes, Mary. With me. Or else return to Maggie Teal's. And end up like Katy.'

'What's the matter with Katy? How do you

66

know her?'

'She's well-known,' he said. 'Most of the lads round here know Katy.'

Suddenly, Mary knew that she had been deluding herself. Of course, she had suspected both Katy and Maggie Teal of no good. She had been blind in her haste to make American shores. It was all becoming disastrously clear. She had fallen into bad hands! A thing that her mother had dreaded above all. Hot tears filled her eyes. She had a sudden desire to run out of the room screaming for the police, but she knew that would do no good.

'It really suits you,' he said. 'I'll see you get to keep it.' He was speaking as if he owned her too. Mary felt very sick now and suddenly afraid. Sean had offered to protect her. But could she believe him? Could she trust him?

She cursed herself for being silly enough to write that letter. For not staying on the island where she was safe. 'Did you know The Shamrock Tree was such a vile place when you came here?' she asked in a low tone. 'Tell me the truth.'

'I did,' was the honest answer.

'Then why did you come? Are you as bad as they are?'

'Believe me, I am not,' Sean answered. 'And I will prove it to you. You must pretend to be with me. That way no one will dare get to you.'

'What do I have to do?' Her heart was beating unreasonably fast. He got up and stood over her, his back to the fire.

'We must pretend,' he repeated. 'You must stay here with me.'

'Stay with you? In your room?' Her whole body trembled at the thought. And not only from fear.

'I promise you'll be safe. Don't worry.' He must have caught her expression of uncertainty. 'You can trust me. You can sleep in my bed and I will have the couch.' Then Sean stooped and put his hands on her shoulders. His eyes seemed honest enough. 'You asked me why I came here? I came to this place on purpose. And not out of choice, seeing as how it's turned out. This is not what I wanted. I made myself a promise that when I reached America, I would conduct my business here as quickly as I could. And then return to Ireland. I can tell you no more. Yet.'

'You want to go back to Ireland?' asked Mary incredulously. 'What is there for you? I thought you were here to make your fortune!'

'I am, but not in the way you think. I hate the city and all it stands for.' Sean spoke with real bitterness and Mary knew exactly what he meant. Like her, he missed green fields and shining water.

New York had been everything Mary wanted, until she arrived and found herself in this mess. Now she would have given anything, faced anyone to be back in the cottage in Brala. But something inside her was still saying, But you'd want him with you, now, wouldn't you?

He seemed close to her now, but there was nothing of the old Sean about him. He was morose, not merry. He looked as if he had a thousand troubles, that he could be a dangerous man. Mary closed her eyes momentarily, praying for guidance.

She wanted to be with him, but she knew that she should not. However, at this moment, Sean Mullen appeared to be her only hope.

CHAPTER SEVEN

'How can I stay here?' Mary asked. 'I have no clothes or belongings with me, except this.' She indicated the blue silk. 'Maggie Teal is keeping my bundles for me.' She remembered how careful the woman had been to say she would keep Mary's things safe. Of course, she was making sure that Mary would return. Everything was beginning to make sense.

'I will see that your bags are fetched,' replied Sean. 'And, as I said before, you must keep the dress. It suits you. It matches the colour of your eyes.' Mary blushed. It was the first real compliment that he had paid her, since they left the ship. Somehow, though, it did not please her.

'I don't want it,' she said quietly. 'It doesn't

belong to me.'

'Don't worry, Mary,' he said quickly, 'One day, I will see that you will have even prettier gowns to wear.'

'I shall work for my own things, Sean Mullen,' she replied sharply. 'No man need buy a dress for me.' Immediately after she was sorry. She realised he meant well by the look in his eyes. For a moment, the old Sean had returned.

'I'm glad to see that your recent misfortunes have not knocked the spirit out of you.' He grinned, then his expression darkened. 'You will keep the dress. Maggie Teal will be glad she gave it to you.'

'What do you mean?'

'Never mind.' He shook his head and drew out a fine, gold watch. Mary gasped inwardly. How had he come by it? 'It is time I was getting down there. Don't open the door to anyone, when I'm gone. And I mean anyone. And get some rest. You look as if you need it.'

'Can we talk when you return?' asked Maggie.

'If you like. There's more bread and cheese, if you're still hungry. I will bring up your things later.' Suddenly, he looked extra solemn. A second later, to her surprise, he took her in his arms. She didn't know what to do and looked away to cover her confusion. 'And don't be thinking of running off, will you?' He was holding her tight.

'Why would I?' she whispered. At that he seemed satisfied and, letting her go, turned towards the door.

'We shall talk,' he said. 'And, remember, don't let anyone in,' he repeated.

'I won't,' she said, going to the door with him.

'Keep the latch down.'

'I will,' she replied. A moment later, he had hurried through and she was all alone in the room. Suddenly, what was happening overtook her and she had to hang on to the table for support, as the room whirled round. She sat down quickly and stared into the fire, like he had.

She could see she was in as much a prison as she had been last night. But now it was with him. The man, who had filled her dreams, on the boat; who had said he'd be her sweetheart. Yet it was all wrong. Besides, the little voice in her head kept insisting, You wanted to leave home, Mary. You wanted to see life, Mary. Now you really are.

Bright tears rushed to her eyes, but she dried them bravely. She had to trust somebody. And, for now, it had to be Sean Mullen . . .

The day passed very slowly. In fact, it was not much different from all those long and weary hours she had passed, waiting for release from Ellis Island. After she had completed the kind of household tasks any woman might in a strange man's room, she sat down and began to think about the plight she was in.

She looked down at the white cotton shirt, which lay on her lap. She had noticed that it had two buttons missing and had nosed about trying to find needle and thread. Surprisingly enough, she found a little work box, with reels and buttons all neatly placed; the kind a woman might possess. As Mary sewed, she fancied he must have had it from his mother. He had never mentioned either of his parents.

Wondering about them had passed another half hour and, although she was a little anxious he mightn't approve, she had set about tidying up his clothes and, ten minutes later, found herself in the embarrassing position of holding a pair of his soft, brown, corduroy breeches, which she stroked into place in one of the large drawers. What was she doing? She hardly knew the lad, who was at that moment keeping her prisoner in his room in a public house.

'What am I doing here?' she asked herself out loud. Her own unnatural reflection stared back. She didn't seem like Mary Flynn any more—and she wasn't in these clothes. They were not hers and they had been borrowed from a woman of ill repute.

Mary shivered. When would Sean return with her things so she could get away? But where would she go? She shook her head hopelessly. Yes, Sean seemed to be her only hope at the present time.

He had not told her when he'd return, nor what he was going to do next with her. Perhaps she should escape right now and find a police station, throwing herself on the mercy of the authorities. Only one thing stopped her. The look in his eyes, the way he'd held her. Her body had flamed to his touch.

Pulling herself together, she busied herself with more household tasks, cooking some food she found in the cupboard. But, by the time she had finished, she didn't feel hungry enough to eat, as her stomach was churning.

Finally, after many glances at the clock on the mantelpiece, she sat down and tried to collect her thoughts. Poor Mary was so much in confusion that she hardly heard the soft knocking on the door. She started up in the chair. 'Who is it?' She'd always been brave, but she was sure her voice was quivering.

'Sure to God, it's Katy Flynn. Let me in, will you!' Mary jumped up, then remembered. Sean had told her not to let anyone in, anyone at all. She stopped and moved away from the door, her mind turning over the possibilities. If Katy was the kind of girl Sean had told her she was, then Mary should obey him.

'What do you want?'

'To see you. Maggie would like the dress back.'

'I can't let you in,' she replied. Silence ensued, and a scuffling outside. She put her ear to the door and heard whispers. Uneasily drawing back, she listened. A moment later, another voice.

'It's Michael Mallon. Let me in, Miss Flynn.' This time, she was afraid. 'I'm sorry, Mr Mallon, Sean told me to let nobody in.'

'Did he, by God,' snarled Mallon. 'Well, miss, this is my property, not his. The lad works for me. I am his landlord. Open the door.' Mary set her chin as she always did when she was determined.

'You must ask Sean, then, sir,' she replied bravely. 'I will not open it.'

'Damn you,' he muttered and, again, she heard low voices. Mary ran across the room and, dragging the heavy chair up to the door, she pushed it against it, then sat down.

She could hear the clink of keys. Then to her horror, she could hear a variety of keys being tried in the lock. Then one fitted. But the bolts were still drawn. And she would not draw them back for the devil himself! The door rattled, as if a great wind was trying to enter.

Mary closed her eyes. What was she going to do?

'What the hell are you doing, Mallon? Get away from the door!' It was Sean! She was safe! She looked up at the ceiling with silent thanks in her heart. 'If you want to see me, I'm here now!' Sean was so strong, so bold.

'Get the girl's clothes off her. Maggie Teal

74

is wanting them back.'

'Maggie may want. But she will only get when I am ready. Back off, Mallon!' She could imagine what was happening. The two would be facing each other out, like they had earlier. There was no love lost between them, so why did Sean work for the man? Why hadn't he found himself a more decent place to live? 'That one will be no good to you, Sean,' spat Mallon.

'Nor to you!' was the response. Then she heard feet hurrying off. A moment later, the key was turning in the lock. She hesitated, as fear had knocked the wind out of her. Then the door was being pushed. Mary swallowed, and jumped off the chair. 'Mary! Are you all right? Draw back the bolts.'

'I am, Sean. Just let me pull the chair away.' A moment later, she had pushed it and the bolts aside. Her saviour entered the room carrying her bundles! She looked at them in relief. Her things were safe.

'You look pale,' he said simply. 'Did they frighten you?'

'A little, but I did as you said Sean.'

'Good girl.' He made no movement towards her, only crossed over to the fire and slumped into the chair. She followed. A moment later, he looked up at her and added passionately, 'I hate this place.' She had never seen such emotion in his face before.

'But why do you stay, Sean?' she asked,

kneeling down beside him. 'We could . . .' She was trying to say what was in her heart, then it came out in a rush. 'We could find some other place, where we're both happy.'

'I can't,' he said dully. 'And I can't tell you why.'

'I don't understand,' cried Mary.

'I have to stay here until . . .' He stopped but was unwilling to give her the explanation she needed.

'Until what?' He shook his head in answer.

'Not now, Mary.' He looked round. 'Why, you've tidied up this old place.'

'And mended your shirt,' she said shyly, knowing that she should not worry him with more questions, however much she needed the answers. 'And put away your things. Have you had your dinner?' He shook his head.

'Have you?'

'I haven't had time,' she lied. In fact, she'd been too busy with her own thoughts to eat the potato soup she had made. She'd also cooked some bacon and cabbage in the frying pan, seasoned it and covered it with a plate, in case he was hungry when he came home. 'Will you take some of the soup I have made, while I change.'

'You have made soup?' he asked, surprised. He went over to the large pan and lifted the lid. 'I've not had home-made soup since I left Kerry.'

'There's some bacon and cabbage too in the

76

other pan. If you don't want it, then we can keep it until tomorrow.'

'What a clever girl you are, Mary,' he said and there was no hint of mockery in his tone. Once again, she thought how Sean Mullen had changed from the devilish lad she had first met on the boat. 'We'll eat some, then we'll take some air.' Her heart leaped at the thought of being free.

'Go out? At this time?' She could hardly believe it.

'You'll be safe with me,' he added reassuringly. 'We'll have a craic. And, maybe, dance.' He smiled, his mood changing completely.

'I can't dance,' she said.

'Then I'll teach you.'

'You know how to dance?'

'I know how to do everything,' he replied, without shyness. Sean had a captivating way about him that reassured her completely. She had thrown in her lot with a man she knew nothing about but, instinctively, Mary knew it had been the right thing to do.

'But I have nothing to wear,' she exclaimed.

'Then keep on what you're wearing now,' he said.

'Oh, no,' she replied quickly. 'This does not belong to me, however beautiful it is.' If she wore the blue dress, it would be like a badge of shame. But a man would probably not understand how she felt.

77

'I could buy another dress for you.'

'No, you could not, Sean. I will not be bought clothes by a man.' She didn't understand the expression that followed, so to cover her confusion, she went to one of her bundles. 'I have something, I think,' she replied.

'Yes, go into the other room and change. I will take your bundles. 'He picked them up and walked over to the door. 'Why, you have tidied up in here too.' He placed her baggage on the bed. 'It's good to have you here, Mary,' he said. She was still standing at the bedroom door. 'I'll go out then,' he said, passing her by so close that it made her feel dizzy.

She closed the bedroom door and rummaged madly in her bundle looking for her very best dress and, drawing it out, surveyed it critically. It looked a poor, crumpled thing, very far removed from the one she was wearing but, however beautiful the blue one was, she did not love it, because it was not hers.

'I can't wear this until it's ironed,' she said out loud. He must have heard her because a step sounded outside the door.

'I have a flat iron,' he said. Sean became more surprising by the minute. She had always known he was deeply mysterious. She longed then to know why he was in this place when he could have run away months ago. But Mary promised herself she'd find out. Maybe

78

tonight?

As she ironed, he was almost his merry self again, talking of what he had done on ship and where he would take her that night. Nothing of his earlier sadness—and Mary spoke nothing about it either.

When she had finished the gingham and it looked tolerably well, Sean went over to the dresser and opened a drawer with a tiny key he took from his pocket. A moment later, he withdrew an expensive-looking box, ornamented with a silver crest. When he brought it out and set it on the table, Mary saw that the crest was the same as the seal he had given her on the ship. She did not like to pry, but was aching to know what was inside.

'Here,' he said, taking out something wrapped in fine tissue. 'It will look nice on your dress.' Mary gasped as she unwrapped the present.

'Oh, it's the finest collar I've ever seen!' A rich, lace collar which would fit wonderfully over her old, pink gingham and make her look like a princess. Where had he come by it? It was evidently of great sentimental value. 'I can't take this, though, I might spoil it.'

'Wear it,' he said. 'Please, Mary, wear it tonight.' She knew then that either it had belonged to a lady, or the servant of a lady. Who else would possess such a beautiful thing?

'Thank you, Sean,' she said, gathering up

the dress and the collar and walking towards the bedroom. Her fear that he might be badly behaved towards her, was receding. How much must he respect her to present her with his mother's lace? Suddenly, Mary was on fire to know more about Sean Mullen and the mystery of his birth, that he kept locked away in that secret box.

*   *   *

To Mary, who had never entered a dance hall before, the place was Heaven with its burning wall lights and stage, complete with band.

Everyone seemed to be laughing around her; there was no stuffiness in comparison with the only proper dancing she had ever seen at the Big House in Brala, when Lady Bennett had held a Christmas ball. All her tenants and servants were allowed to watch the proceedings from a distance and, to Mary as a child, the ladies in their wonderful coloured dresses, whirling around the floor, seemed like angels.

But that fine company had not danced to music like Mary heard issuing from the door of the dance hall she entered on Sean Mullen's arm, conscious that many jealous pairs of eyes swivelled in her direction. Why not? breathed Mary to herself, After all, I shall be dancing with the handsomest man there.

She had told him she could not dance, but

the music was the kind she had heard in the village back home, the high pitched fiddle and the beat of the drum.

'Why, I can do this,' she said soon, looking up at him. 'It's a reel!' And next moment, they were dashing into the fray and Mary was swung high off her feet many a time as she moved from partner to partner.

Breathlessly she finally landed beside Sean again, who took her over to a small table and bought her sweet lemonade in a tall glass.

'Can we talk now?' she asked, looking into his eyes,

'You like dancing, Mary?' he asked, his eyes roving over her face. She hoped she looked well, knowing she had lost her heart to him already.

'It's exciting,' she said, 'but . . . but I would like to hear about you, Sean.'

'What do you want me to say?' he asked.

'More than you did on the ship,' she replied. 'Tell me about the seal—and you being descended from high folks.'

'Did I say that?'

'You did. Don't pretend you didn't. And I still have your seal.' She withdrew it from its secret place under her clothes. 'What did you mean?' she persisted. She saw him swallow as if he was about to speak, but all he did, was to lean back in his chair and regard her steadily. 'Are you thinking that you can't trust me?' she asked indignantly. 'I trusted you.'

'That you did, Mary Flynn,' He nodded slowly. 'I was only thinking that it might be the worse for you, if you did know.'

'You have tell me now!' she said. 'Stop teasing me.' He smiled and his face lit up, then became serious again. He leaned forward and so did she.

'All right, but it's a sad tale, mind.'

'I'm ready,' she replied, although her hands were sweating. 'Go on.'

'I came to America, not only to make my fortune—which I may never do—but to find . . .' he stopped, as if what he was saying was causing him real pain, then added, '. . . to find my father.'

'Your father,' Mary repeated.

'Aye,' he said shortly. 'I knew he was in New York and I had heard that he frequented the hell-hole known as The Shamrock Tree.'

'But who told you?' cried Mary.

'The folks that adopted me.'

'You're adopted?'

'That I am,' said Sean and his voice was hard. 'I know who my mother is, but I do not know much about my father. She is a lady— still alive—who brought me, as a baby, to those people I called my parents until I was twenty-one, when the truth was disclosed by them that I was not their real son.'

'How terrible!' said Mary. 'Why were they so cruel?'

'They had been paid, God love them. They

had no option. They were poor people, who did what they were told. Now how do you feel about me? I'm a bastard, Mary.' Real pain showed in his eyes. She reached out instinctively and covered his hand with hers.

'It's not your fault,' she said. 'How could your mother desert you?'

'She was made to by her husband.' Mary gasped. 'Yes, she was a married woman, who was taken in by my scandalous father. A lady, who was forced to give me up for decency's sake. All I know of her is that she loved me.' He put a hand to his brow as if to push away the memory. 'She left me her seal to remember me by and my foster parents told me that the last words she said, when she abandoned me to them, were, 'One day I will come for my boy and he will claim his rightful inheritance.'

'She would send regular money for my keep, as I think he did sometimes.'

'Then he must not have been all bad.'

'He left me, didn't he? And her to face the music.'

All Mary could think at that moment was that Sean had entrusted her with his precious seal. And that she had been right about the collar she was wearing. She felt dizzy at the thought of how much he must care; although he had never said so, except when they were on the ship together. Maybe there was such a thing as love at first sight.

'Your mother might come to find you yet,' she said, attempting to soothe him. 'Did she live far from you?'

'A county away.'

'How did she choose your parents?'

'You ask a lot of questions, Mary,' he said.

She blushed. 'I just want to know as much as I can about you.'

'She came from Cork. Your county.'

'Did she tell your foster parents who your father was?' Most people knew each other in Cork.

'I know nothing about him except that once or twice he got in touch with them and sent money to keep me, as I told you. They had to take it, poor souls. They scorned him for the blackguard he was; for what he had done to an innocent woman. And those letters always came from The Shamrock Tree. Someone knows something here and I intend to find it out. One day I know I'll meet him and then . . .' He stopped.

'And then what will you do? Are you out to get revenge, Sean Mullen?'

'What do you think?' he asked.

'I think it will do little good,' replied Mary wisely. 'He must have suffered himself over the years to know that he had lost a woman he loved and his son.'

'I know he didn't love her!' burst out Sean, striking his fist so hard on the table that other people sitting by looked round. 'My foster parents said that the man was a blackguard. His feckless ways had been the talk of the town. I was born in pain and sorrow.

'Why am I telling you this?' he asked, almost to himself.

'Why are you then?' asked Mary, knowing how much she wanted to hear the right answer. It seemed that she had grown-up years since the first time she had set foot on American shores.

'I'm not sure,' he replied, disengaging his hand and resting his head on his two arms for several moments. She glanced around to see who might be looking but, at that moment, the band struck up a merry jig. He lifted his head and, to her surprise, his dark eyes looked bright as if he was about to weep. Instead, he grimaced ruefully and asked, 'Shall we dance?'

As Mary was whirled light-footed through the paces, Sean twisting her strongly in his arms, she was dizzy, not only from the dance, but also from confusion. When they finally left in the soft darkness of the early summer evening, all Mary could think about was the sad tale he'd related and her own happy feelings that he had shared his secret with her.

She wondered as they walked in silence arm-in-arm along the pavement, whether her mother might have heard the story of the lady from Cork, who had been bewitched by some no-good Irish lad, who had disappeared off to America leaving his lover in the lurch. Ireland was a small place and each county knew everything about the goings-on within it.

She also couldn't forget that anger on Sean's face as he had told her how he would find his father whatever happened, but what was most surprising of all was that he wanted to go back to the Old Country. It seemed that Mary had grown up over the last few weeks and that, even now, she was thinking that perhaps Ireland was not a bad place to bring up a family, as long as you had a job, of course.

She felt her face flame in the darkness. What are you thinking of, Mary Flynn, spinning such tales in your head? she asked herself. Sean has never asked you to marry him after he finds his father.

'Are you tired after all that jigging?' he asked.

'No,' she murmured.

'You're very quiet.'

'I was thinking—about home,' she added.

'Is Brala a good place to live?' he asked suddenly.

'Tolerable,' she replied. 'I couldn't get out fast enough at first, but now . . .' she paused, '. . . now I can see some of its good points.'

'Tell me,' he said. 'I would like to know all about it.' Soon, she was telling him about the Big House and Lady Bennett and how she had given Mary the money to take ship to her aunt. Sean seemed very interested and asked lots of questions about the village itself, which was part of the English lord's estate.

Before long, they were standing at the entrance to The Shamrock Tree. 'I don't want to take you back in here, Mary,' Sean said, looking down into her eyes.

'I shall come to no harm,' she replied, knowing she had him to protect her.

'I can't look out for you all the time,' he said, as if he was reading her thoughts. 'But I want you to stay with me longer.'

'Do you? What will everyone think?'

'Nobody thinks anything here,' he said bitterly. 'Girls come in and out daily.'

Looking into those deep, dark eyes of his, she would be a fool to imagine he was a saint. She knew then that he might have had a hundred girls but, somewhere, inside, she felt that, if he had, it wouldn't have mattered to her, as long as he didn't have any more now.

'Then I'll stay with you, Sean.' She smiled. 'In any case, I have nowhere else to go.' A moment later, he had hold of her arm quite firmly.

'What I told you tonight, must go no further than you and me. I want no one to know my business.'

'Don't you trust me, Sean? But your secret is safe.'

'How could I do otherwise?' he asked, 'with those blue eyes looking up so earnestly into mine? I believe you, Mary and, when I find that no-good father of mine, things will be

87

different between us.'

'What do you mean?' Her voice trembled a little.

'I can make you no promises now,' he replied, 'but I shall have to kiss you, if you keep looking at me like that.'

A moment later, she felt his strong lips on hers and gave no resistance. She felt as if he was drawing out her very soul, which flew to meet his own with a swiftness that surprised her. She abandoned herself entirely to him.

Those two other kisses they had shared had been nothing like this one—that first brief one on the ship had been nothing, nor had the hard way that he had kissed her in front of Mallon any comparison. He kissed her that night as if he really loved her.

A moment later, they broke apart and she found herself trembling. 'You make a man shiver, Mary,' he said.

'Do I?' Her head was as dizzy now, as it had been from dancing. But the spell was immediately broken because, a moment later, a voice rudely broke them apart. It was Mallon, who hammered on the door and pushed them over the threshold.

'You'll have plenty of time for this, lad, when you get to bed,' the boss said roughly. Mary blushed.

'Keep a civil mouth in front of her,' snarled Sean.

'I'll do as I please in my own pub,' retorted

the landlord. 'Now if you want to keep your place here, you'll quit canoodling and do some work—both of you.'

The ragged-looking urchin, who had opened the door to her when Mary had arrived first with Katy, grinned at them from his seat by the door.

'Why. What suitable job could she do here?' asked Sean. 'I'll not have her working behind the bar. Nor in the kitchen.'

'Choosy, aren't you, Sean?' sneered Mallon. 'She's a fine-looking wench. She can sit at the door and attend to the customers. Will that suit you? If she was your wife, I would expect no less.'

'I'll do it, sir,' said Mary. 'No—Sean, I will. I have to earn my keep.'

'Who said I was going to pay you?' asked Mallon, nastily.

'If you don't, then I shan't do it,' replied Mary decidedly.

Both men were staring now.

'Some spirit there, lad,' said Mallon.

'I'll not have anyone touch her, mind,' Sean stated.

'No one will touch me, or they'll feel the weight of my tongue,' said Mary. 'Where do I sit?' The next moment, Mallon delivered a kick at the boy by the door.

'Get off that stool,' he said, 'and let this fine woman take over.'

'I don't like it,' said Sean.

'If you don't, you know what you can do, Mullen.'

'I'll do it, I said,' cried Mary. 'Who's to come in?'

'There's a list, but,' began Mallon, producing it from his pocket, 'it's only of use if you can read.'

'I can,' replied Mary. 'Can he?' The boy was hovering, evidently hoping Mary would tail.

'Jimmy keeps it all in his head. But he makes a hell of a lot of mistakes.' Mallon glowered as the boy smiled proudly.

'Then I will read who comes, and Jimmy can keep them in order.'

'Just like a woman. Taking charge,' said Mallon. 'That's why I have no wife.' Still, there was a note of admiration in his voice. 'Can you do sums as well?'

'I have a great head for figures.' She could see that he was about to make some ribald remark, but changed his mind in front of Sean.

'Then if you do well, I'll be taking you on as my secretary. How would that suit you, Sean?' He didn't reply.

A moment later, Mallon stalked off. Then a sharp rap sounded on the door. 'Well, get on with it then, Mary Flynn,' said Jimmy.

'Don't be so cheeky,' snapped Sean and the boy looked afraid.

'Don't worry, I'll be all right,' she said. 'Jimmy will help, won't you?' The urchin nodded.

'I'll be back if you need me.'

'I know. Now go on.' A minute later, the boy was opening the door a crack.

'Who is it?' A muttered response followed and next moment, Mary was consulting the list Mallon had provided.

As the night wore on, Mary had little time to think as there were many callers at The Shamrock, some silent, reckless-looking men, who appeared to be not of good character, come looking for Mallon and led off by Jimmy; others, only tired, working men, seeking some refuge from their labour in The Shamrock's beer, who spoke to her kindly enough and in a gentlemanly-like way.

However, others were wanting to speak to her too much and, once or twice, Sean appeared from nowhere to send them packing. It was good that he was keeping an eye on her for, occasionally, Mary felt afraid and wished she were back in Brala.

Sometimes, when she had a second to breathe, she could hardly believe that she had come all the way to New York to run a decent boarding house with her aunt and had ended up as a porter in a common public house. But then the thought of Sean's kiss swept away all her fears and, when the pub closed, going back to his rooms as if they were man and wife.

CHAPTER EIGHT

But they were not man and wife! How keenly Mary felt that every morning she awoke early and listened to the sound of him stirring next door. He had kept his word and stayed out of the bedroom and, after a week or so, she was trusting him with everything.

Sometimes, if he was on very early, he would come into her with a steaming mug of tea. He seemed the most handsome when he was the most dishevelled, in his nightshirt, with the dark stubble on his face, where he had not shaved. She was glad that he did not wear a moustache like Mallon, or a beard like her father. She liked smooth-faced men. She was beginning to find out more about him too. What he liked, what he ate, but not what was his work or where he went.

Only once had his face darkened, when she probed too deeply as to what he did for Mallon. 'You do your job and I will do mine, Mary. Hopefully, neither of them will last too long.' Sometimes, she wondered what went on under that dark thatch of hair and those eyes, which could be so very hard sometimes, and then so soft with her.

All she had gleaned of his work was that he was Michael Mallon's right-hand man, which was strange as he was the least like any man that worked in The Shamrock Tree or any that visited there. The only way in which he resembled his boss was that he wore the same dark suit and a high collar, almost as if he was a gentleman.

But wasn't he that really, Mary thought as he left her to drink her tea. Nothing improper had taken part between them privately since that last wonderful kiss, but the woman in Mary knew that they were both holding back until the right time. But how long would that be, when she was desperate for him to join her in his bed, but she knew it would be wrong.

Neither of them had spoken recently about going to find out if her Aunt Flynn had perished in the fire. As the days passed, Mary had also felt that she should write to her mother to let her know what was happening, but what would she say about where she was. On the other hand, her mother would be mad for news.

In the end, she sent off the letter feeling very guilty. In it, Mary had written that she had met a female companion on ship, with whom she was staying at present; also that she was doing a decent job and that she would write again soon. She also added the sad news that Aunt Flynn had never come to fetch her and that she may have died in a fire.

Next, she filled up the letter with nonsense about the excitement of being in New York and what a wonderful place it had turned out to be. At least, that was not a lie. It was wonderful being with the man she knew she loved. But she'd had to lie about her residence, so she gave Maggie Teal's address instead.

By now, Maggie had held off, thinking that she and Sean were engaged, which gave Mary a status at The Shamrock Tree. She'd been so right when she'd first suspected no one played games with, or put down Sean Mullen.

'Maggie says you can use the address,' Katy had told her one evening, 'but she says you must pay her for the privilege.'

'I'll ask Sean,' replied Mary sweetly. She wasn't feeling very saint-like at the time. Katy looked startled and Mary knew she would carry the message back. In one way, she was sorry for the girl, being pawed over by men, but she was only too glad that the same fate had not befallen her. She thanked God every day that she had met Sean on the ship, otherwise what would have become of her?

But when would they get away from this awful place? She was thinking so one morning when Sean brought her tea once more. He was washed, dressed and wearing his suit. 'You're up early,' she said brightly.

He paused, then replied, 'Mary, something is going to happen today.'

'What do you mean happen?' She was almost afraid of his look. It was a mixture of apprehension and fear—and she didn't like to see Sean afraid. It made her frightened too.

'It's what I've been waiting for, girlie,' he said, going over to the window and looking out. She didn't speak, knowing he'd tell her if he wanted to. He turned, 'Today—I shall know who my father is.'

'Oh Sean, how?' she cried, jumping out of bed in excitement. He shrugged as she stood before him in her nightgown and then smiled.

'Don't jig about so.'

'Sorry!' She felt young and naive, in front of this dark man, whose face was suddenly full of care. 'I was only excited for you.'

'I know. You asked me how.' She nodded. 'I have had spies out for a long time. The fellow's name is O'Mara. He came over on the boat with my father. It has taken a long time to find him. I have had to pay for his railway ticket. He was out in Boston.' Sean's sentences were brief, as if he couldn't wait to get away and speak to the man.

'Who are your spies?' The question came suddenly.

'Why did you ask me that, girlie?' He looked at her keenly. Mary knew she shouldn't have said it. He would think she'd been prying. But they were supposed to have no secrets.

'I only wondered how you found him.'

'It was one of the shopkeepers I visit, whose brother told him.' So he visited shopkeepers. She didn't know that was his business.

'Where are you going to meet this O'Mara?'

'Now that's a bit difficult, Mary. I'm relying

95

on you to help me on that one.'

'What can I do?' She'd have done anything to take that look off his face. She was so afraid that he was going to murder someone. And then where would they be? Would she be strong enough to stop him doing something silly when he did find his father? He was so hot-tempered—a real Irish temper he had. She had seen enough instances already in the week she had been there.

'You are the doorkeeper, my darling.' He had never called her that before. It was almost as though he was having to bribe her to do so, when she would have done anything for him readily. She could see that the only thing that mattered to him most in the world was getting O'Mara into the pub without Mallon knowing. No stranger came to The Shamrock Tree without an invitation.

'You can't ask the boss then?'

'No, I don't want him to know what I really came here for. I can show no weakness.' He sat down on the bed and put his head in his hands.

'You're not weak,' exclaimed Mary. 'Why, you're the strongest man I know. Everyone is afraid of you and takes notice of what you say.' He looked up and she didn't understand his expression.

'Are you afraid of me, Mary?'

'Of course not.'

'You might be if . . .' He broke off.

'If . . . what?' Mary was very puzzled and, in spite of what she'd just said, more than a little frightened.

'If you knew what I did.'

'You can tell me, Sean,' she said, sitting down on the bed beside him.

'I'm afraid to.' She couldn't believe what she'd just heard.

'Why?'

'You may not like me any more.'

She smiled. How could she not like him? She was in love with him. 'Whatever you do.' She swallowed. 'Or have done, won't make any difference to how I feel about you, Sean Mullen. You know that.'

'Do I?' She nodded.

'Try me.' He looked away. Then at her again.

'I found out about O'Mara, because I . . . put the screws on a shopkeeper.'

'I don't understand.'

'How could you?' Sean laughed bitterly. 'Mary, I am Mallon's unwilling servant. I go about collecting money for him every week and for that, I offer those poor people some protection from . . .' He shrugged hopelessly. 'From anyone who wants to muscle in on this small patch of Irish territory, be he Italian, Jewish, or any other nation under the sun. Now do you understand what I do, Mary?' He hung his head.

'How did you get into this, Sean?' asked

97

Mary. 'And so quickly. Why did you come here? Why did you agree?'

'I told you why I came. To find my father. And Mallon just . . . seemed to take a shine to me. He must have seen what I was really like. He saw I was like him.'

'No, Sean, you're good and kind.'

'I am neither.' He turned sad eyes on her face. 'It is only you who can see the good in me.'

'I wouldn't be able to see it, if it wasn't there,' insisted Mary. 'I can't excuse what you do, but I think I understand. At least, I'm trying to.' Neither of them spoke for a moment afterwards. Both were thinking their own thoughts. Mary didn't know what Sean's were, but her own were a mixture of horror and disbelief that the man she had grown to love could behave like that. Worst of all, part of her could see that he would be good at it. That was why nobody at The Shamrock ever crossed him. Even his own boss Mr Mallon.

'I knew this is what would happen,' he said suddenly. 'That is why I never told you before. I can see by your face that you're shocked and I don't blame you.'

'I am,' she said finally. 'But I know you hate what you have to do and that must be a good sign—it shows that you are not all bad. After you meet O'Mara, and maybe, find out who your father is, you will not have to do such work any more. You can leave here. You can

98

be at peace.'

'Bless you, Mary,' he said, taking her hand and holding it to his lips. 'You don't hate me then?'

'Of course I don't.' She swallowed, finding her mouth had gone very dry. 'You've not had to hurt people, have you?'

'I have not had to,' he said. 'That is the truth. Most of Mallon's clients are afraid of me.'

'Thank God for that,' she said. 'I wouldn't want to be married to a thug.' He looked at her with wondering eyes. 'Do you know what you just said?'

'I do.' A moment later, he had her caught in his arms and was swinging her off her feet as he had done in the dance hall.

'And you will not, dear girl, I promise. I will reform and be a model husband.' So it was all out. It was not the way Mary had thought a proposal to her would ever come. But it had, and she was happy—happy it had happened.

Mary was almost too happy as she sat down and listened to Sean's instructions regarding O'Mara. She could hardly believe that, finally, he had committed himself to her and now she had to hope that nothing would go wrong.

Although, later, that evening, when she was seated in her usual place by the door, she began to think of her dadda and what he would have made of Sean Mullen. Would he have thought him a rascal? Of course he would. Maybe he would have forbidden her to marry a bad young man. He certainly would not have approved of his present way of life. But Mary would have brought him round, pleading that Sean was good inside and only doing what he did until he found his father . . .

'What are you thinking of, Mary?' asked little Jimmy, who was perched beside her stool on another. 'You look all lighted-up inside.'

'Thank you, Jimmy,' said Mary. 'That was a very nice compliment from a lad, who didn't want me to take his job. But we make a good team now, don't we? By the way, is Mr Mallon in this evening?'

'He is not,' replied Jimmy. 'He told me to give you tonight's list. It is short and you can go off early when you've done. He'll see you about tomorrow's.' Mary breathed a sigh of relief. It was just how Sean had said it would be and the coast would be clear for O'Mara and Sean to meet and talk.

The next thing was to get Jimmy out of the way. That was her job. She and the boy had become friends and Mary could feel that he had something of a crush upon her.

Jimmy was an orphan and had no one to turn to. He had come over on a ship with his brother, who had been crushed loading crates in the docks. Mallon had taken the little lad to live at The Shamrock and so earn his keep.

The rough girls, who frequented the place, poked fun at him, while a lot of the customers

100

made him fetch and carry for them endlessly, but Mary was sorry for him and always gave him a kind word. She didn't like using him for her own purposes but desperate measures needed desperate remedies sometimes. She had already decided what to do . . .

As the appointed time approached, she said to Jimmy nonchalantly, 'I would do anything for a bagel.'

'Don't you want cabbage and bacon tonight then, Mary?'

'No, I have had enough of it for the time being. I could really do with one of Miss Esther's bagels.' Miss Esther's was a Jewish baker's shop a good half a mile up the block. Sean had taken Mary there once and they'd had a mouthwatering feast. 'Will you do this for me, Jimmy?'

'I suppose so, Mary.' The boy looked doubtful.

'You know where it is? Off 25th.' Jimmy nodded. 'If you will fetch me—three—you can have one.' His face brightened considerably at the bribe. 'You can choose yours, but see that mine has Esther's special cream cheese.'

Then Mary produced the money with a flourish. 'I hope I can trust you not to eat the lot. Nor to get run over!'

'I'm not a baby,' burst out the boy, 'but what would the boss say, if he knew I was going on errands for you?'

'Well, he won't know, will he?' urged Mary.

'He's not here. Can't a girl get tired of bacon, cabbage and stew?'

'All right, Mary, I'll be quick.' Jimmy grabbed his cap and was gone like a streak of light. Mary glanced at her fob. It was time. She looked round and could see Sean standing in the bar doorway, his tall, lean frame outlined against the light. He smiled. She nodded back, closed her eyes momentarily and a throb of pride ran through her frame. Every girl in New York would be jealous of her, if they knew she was marrying that lad.

She glanced at the fob again. No sign yet of O'Mara. Sean had no description of him. He would give his name and she would send him straight over. Her heart jumped two or three times in the next ten minutes. Two men arrived off Mallon's list, who tried to flirt with her, then caught Sean's piercing look and moved off quickly. She looked round helplessly and shook her head. If O'Mara didn't hurry up, then Jimmy would be back.

A moment later, she was conscious of a different kind of noise coming from the street. An ugly thud, like the report from a gun, followed by several women's screams and a hum of voices, rising over the traffic.

Gathering up her skirts, she jumped up from her stool and peered out through the trap in the door and, to her surprise, could see nothing except a press of people's backs and shoulders jammed right up against The

102

Shamrock's wall, clamouring and pushing each other, trying to see and trying to move away. 'What's going on?' she cried. 'What's happening?'

Then a man turned and gabbled into her face. 'Some poor lad's been killed on the street.'

Mary's heart suddenly lurched. Could it be little Jimmy? He never took any care, dodging in and out of the noisy traffic dangerously.

A moment later, Sean came striding up. 'Someone's been hurt, but I can't see who it is.' Mary shrugged helplessly. She followed as he let himself out into the crowd, which parted, as he pushed through, to reveal, not Jimmy, but a middle-aged man with grey hair lying crumpled, face down in the street. Her eyes were fixed upon the dull stain which was spreading over the back of the man's jacket, and her hands went up to her face to hide the view.

'Stay back!' Sean ordered. He knelt down and taking a small glass from out of his waistcoat pocket, turned the man slightly over and held the glass to the victim's mouth. Then he put his ear to the man's chest. He sat back on his heels and grimaced.

'I know a doctor,' someone said.

'He's no use of a doctor now,' said Sean. A hush fell on the crowd. 'Does anyone recognise him?' The crowd was dispersing fast. Sean grabbed one of them. 'Did anyone see what happened?' Those curious ones, who were left, shook their heads and crossed themselves.

A moment later, Sean was bending forward again and going through his pockets. Mary watched it all as if she was standing in a dream. She would never forget the expression on Sean's face as he straightened and looked her full in the eyes. He was white and almost shaking himself.

She approached and putting her arm around him, while trying not to look at the corpse, she asked, 'Who is it, Sean?'

'It's O'Mara,' he breathed, 'his name is in his pocket-book.' He still had it open in his hand; then, remembering himself, he put it back and it was then that Mary noticed his hands were covered in blood.

'What happened to him?' she asked, trembling.

'It looks as though he's been shot in the back, girlie,' said another voice. She looked up. It was a policeman. Sergeant O'Brien, a regular visitor to The Shamrock. Mary's head whirled. She felt numb. O'Mara had been shot. 'Do either of you know the fellow?' Both shook their heads instinctively. 'He doesn't come from round here,' added Sean.

'Is that right, Sean Mullen? Are you turning detective now?' added the policeman. Mary shivered.

'She was on the door and I was inside. We

came out when we heard all the commotion and shouting.'

'Can any of you corroborate that?' asked the constable.

'Yes.' Mary and Sean spoke together.

'Yes, I can too, Sergeant.' Mary gasped at the recognisable deep voice. It was Michael Mallon! But he wasn't supposed to be here. He was standing looking down at O'Mara.

'Very well, sir. I'll speak to you two later. And the rest of you. You get inside, miss. You look ready to faint.' Sean took Mary's arm and led her in through the pub door. With a brief gesture, he put a finger to his lips and sat her down.

Next moment, he was offering her some strong drink from a flask in his pocket. Then Mallon stepped over the threshold.

'Not a pretty sight,' he said, looking at Sean. 'You'd better get that blood washed off. And you, Mary, take yourself off too. Where's that little scamp?'

'I sent him on an errand,' replied Mary. The last thing she wanted was for Mallon to take it out on Jimmy. She was responsible.

'Here I am,' said a voice and Jimmy came through the door with the bagels. 'Give me those,' ordered Mallon in a rough voice.

'No, they're mine,' replied Mary. 'I gave him the money.'

'Bacon and cabbage not good enough for you then?' asked Mallon, taking the bag from the boy.

'Give them back to her!' said Sean in a tight, dangerous voice. The men faced each other, then Mallon laughed and thrust the bag into Mary's hands.

'I think they'll be wasted tonight by the look on your pale faces,' he sneered. 'If the police come asking about the man, we've never seen him.'

'We haven't,' replied Sean.

'That's right, we haven't,' said Mallon and walked off. A moment later, Mary was thrusting the three bagels into Jimmy's hands.

'You can have them all. I couldn't eat a thing,' she said, sitting down on the stool. She felt nauseous. Someone had been shot outside the door and that someone was the only person who could have helped Sean in his quest. What were they going to do now? And who could have killed him?

CHAPTER NINE

The Police called into The Shamrock later and took statements from them both. Mallon was present during this ordeal and, all the time Mary was speaking, he had his eyes fixed on her, which made her feel dreadfully uncomfortable. It was as if he knew that she had something to hide.

After the sergeant put away his notebook and dismissed his constable, Mallon started asking questions. O'Brien was a law officer who spent a fair amount of time in The Shamrock himself, although his wife didn't know how friendly he was with some of the young ladies, including Katy. Mallon had got himself on the good side of the law in spite of his doubtful practices, giving the police a backhander wherever he could.

As Sean had said, Mallon made a dangerous enemy, having the wherewithal to get any innocent fellow convicted.

'Who was the stiff, Sergeant?' Mallon's way of asking showed he hadn't an ounce of sympathy in his body. Mary wanted to scream out that Mr O'Mara probably had a wife and children here or back in Ireland who had been depending upon him. She still hadn't got over seeing a man shot in the back.

'Well, he's been identified as a Mr O'Mara from the Boston area. He was a very long way from home. Now I wonder what his business could have been round here,' asked O'Brien in return. Mallon shrugged.

'New York is full of wandering idlers,' he replied, taking a cigar and clenching it between his teeth. 'O'Brien?' He offered the policeman another.

'Not now, but I'll take it home, sir, for afterwards,' replied O'Brien, smelling it, then placing it carefully in his pocket.

'Was there nothing to connect him to this place? Was he here on business, do you think?' The policeman shook his head.

'He was no business man, sir, like you. His clothes and demeanour put him down as a labourer. But he had an appointment to keep. It was written down on a piece of a notepaper. Indeed, he had . . .' The policeman drew in a deep breath, as if he was preparing himself for the next statement. Mary felt herself trembling all over. What if O'Mara had given Sean away by writing down his name?

'. . . he had an appointment with someone connected to this very establishment.' Mallon didn't look surprised. Mary held her breath and did not dare look at Sean, but she could feel a tiny movement in his muscles.

'Indeed. Dye hear that, Sean? The poor man had a meeting here. Now can you think of anyone who would be meeting a labourer from Boston in my pub?'

'I cannot,' replied Sean and his voice was strong.

'What about you, Mary?'

'Leave her out of this.'

'You're always jumping to her defence, Sean.'

'I'm engaged to her. And, anyway, Mary knows no one in Boston.' Mary nodded her head forcefully to corroborate the statement.

'So, sergeant, we have a mystery. A man is killed outside my front door and he was evidently coming to meet one of my customers.'

The sergeant nodded. 'This will have to go to higher authority, Mr Mallon, seeing it is murder.'

'Indeed, it must and I shall be pleased to help anyone of that sort to the best of my ability,' replied Mallon suavely. 'As will anyone employed by me.'

'Thank you, sir,' replied the policeman, 'But I'm fairly sure that no one from The Shamrock is implicated in the crime.' He winked.

'Good! That's it then. Now, won't you take a glass sergeant?'

'I'm on duty, sir,' answered Sergeant O'Brien regretfully.

'Then you must come in tonight and I will get Katy to look after you.'

'Thank you!' The sergeant looked delighted. Mary felt as if she could have screamed at that moment but, sensibly, she kept her lips tightly closed. 'Now, Mary,' said Mallon, 'you're looking grim. I think it must have been the shock. What's more, after this, you won't be placed at the door. It's no seat for a young lady. That young rapscallion, Jim, can take over.'

'But what shall I do then?' She looked across at Sean.

'You write a fair hand; you read admirably and I think now is the time to make you my secretary.' Sean looked at Mallon as if he might kill him. But what could she do but agree?

'I'd like that,' she replied falsely and her voice shook a little.

'She's a smart lass,' added the policeman, his eyes roving over her figure.

'Get you up to my office then,' Mallon ordered. 'I shall follow directly. As for you, Sean, you'd better set about my business.' Mallon's lip curled. He knew he had his way at last. Sean could do nothing with the policeman present. What he might do afterwards was nobody's business!

Mary stood uncertainly in the middle of the room, wondering what she had got herself into. There was something about Mallon that made her flesh creep. She had hoped so much to be free of The Shamrock and all its horrors it entailed—free to be with Sean and not to have to worry about herself or him.

What would they do now? How long would they stay? Sean had said he must find out about his father. She could see by his eyes when he said it, that nothing would sway him from his purpose. They were trapped.

A few minutes later, Mallon strode into the room and, giving her a wide berth, went over and sat behind his desk. He motioned her to sit down on the chair in front of it and began to open drawers and withdraw papers.

She sat motionless. She had made up her mind by then that she would allow him no

110

freedoms. She would keep her distance but, what was most upsetting was that, if he did try anything, she wouldn't dare tell Sean for fear of what he might do. Her love might even end up with a bullet in his back too!

'Well, Mary,' said Mallon, 'cat got your tongue?'

'No, Mr Mallon.'

'Good. One thing I'd like you to know. I intend to give you enough work to keep you out of mischief. How do you feel about that?'

'It's what I want,' replied Mary truthfully.

'Good. But you can do one thing for me, if you will.' His voice was quiet.

'What's that, sir?' Mary could feel little trickles of sweat run in her hair, like tiny snakes wriggling on her head. What was coming?

'I'd like you to tell me about dear old Cork sometimes.' She was startled at the request and, for a moment, didn't know what to say. 'What's the matter? You come from there, don't you?'

'I do,' she said, in a small voice. 'But not from Cork itself.'

'Then where?' he asked.

'From Brala. It's a village outside the town.' How she wished she was there at the moment! But then she wouldn't have met Sean!

'Brala, is it?' He looked very interested. 'Is it a large place?' For some reason, he was evidently trying to be nice to her.

111

'Very small.'

'And what does your father do?' The question was sharp now.

'My father is dead, but he used to work the sea and the land.'

'And what was his name?'

'Conor Flynn.' She was determined she would not let him see how it upset her to talk about her beloved dadda.

'Conor Flynn,' he repeated thoughtfully. Then he rose from his chair and, to her horror, came round and laid a hand on her shoulder.

'I'm sorry that he's dead. And your mother?'

'She married again.'

'To whom?' He was still holding her shoulder.

'To a man called Odone, who works at the Big House.'

'I see.' To her great relief, he let her go. 'So they didn't want you at home with them, then?'

'Something like that,' she lied, watching him carefully, as he returned to his side of the desk. She wondered if she should have lied before too and told him she had come from Cork itself but, surely, it was no harm to tell him the truth. After all, he had never been to her village and, if he had, he would surely find out she was lying.

'That's all the questions for now, Mary,' he said. She swallowed. 'There is a method in my madness, if you can call it that.' He laughed. 'I like to know my trusted employees. So, if they should commit any crime, then I am in the position to inform the authorities.'

'Crime?' asked Mary faintly.

'Well, if you are to be my secretary, you will be handling material of importance. Private accounts and the like. Money, Mary! Money. That's what The Shamrock means. My little empire is as important to me as any in the world. You must learn how to keep your mouth shut. Like Sean.' At that he took out what looked like an account book. 'Now, I would like you to start on these figures.' He came round again and explained what she had to do. All the time she was conscious of his cigar-laden breath on her face.

'Do you understand?' he asked, when he'd finished.

'Yes, sir.' It seemed quite easy. She'd always had a head for book learning.

'I thought you would. You're a clever girl, Mary and clever girls do not get mixed up in things that are underhand. Do you take my meaning?'

'Certainly, Mr Mallon.' She realised then that he did know something and that her earlier fears were founded.

'Now get on with your work. I'll be back later. When you've finished, have a look at those too.' He handed her a much fatter book. 'Those accounts need an eye casting over them.'

'Yes, sir.'

'And, remember, Mary,' he said, crossing the room and opening the door. 'Keep out of things that don't concern your pretty head. Your young man is headstrong. Perhaps you can bring some order to the chaos of his life.' With a meaningful look on his face, Mallon disappeared.

Mary wanted to cry then. There was no doubt in her mind that the boss knew about Sean's enterprise. Maybe he had found out about O'Mara too! It was a frightening thought. In fact, she wanted to rush out of the office at that very moment, find Sean and warn him. But she knew that it wasn't safe.

She looked down at the figures, that danced before her eyes. She felt unsteady and hung on to the chair and, then, reminding herself that she was Mary Flynn from Brala, who was made of sterner stuff, she turned her attention to the task in hand, as she had always done in times of crisis. As soon as she finished with these numbers, it would be time to finish for the day and then go back to their rooms and talk it over with Sean.

But as her pencil soared up and down the columns, checking and rechecking, it came into her mind that Mallon must have something up his sleeve regarding Mary herself. Why did he want to know about her origins? And especially her father?

Finally, she put down her pencil and leaned back against the chair, sighing. It had been a hard day. She was hungry and tired. The money she had given Jim for the bagels had been wasted and she was nigh on fainting.

Getting up, she closed the books and going round the desk, put them away carefully. There was no lock to secure them in the drawer. Doubtless he'd be back to do so. And she wanted to be gone before he did.

A moment later, she was scurrying down the corridor towards the steps. On the way down she met Mallon. She felt more secure in the open. She was sure he would not try anything there. He was blocking her way.

'I've finished all the figures, Mr Mallon and I have put the books away,' she said submissively. She had found that was the best way with him.

'Have you?' he asked.

'There was no key to lock them up.'

'Would I be likely to leave you a key so you could be looking in my private drawers?' he asked and she caught the sarcasm.

'I would not expect you to,' she replied bravely. 'May I go through? I am tired and hungry.' To her utter relief, he stood aside.

'And be here sharp at seven o'clock tomorrow,' he said.

'I will, sir.' She slipped by but, as she hurried down the steps, she could feel his eyes boring into her back and gave an involuntary shiver.

Mallon was hungry too, but not for bagels.

Sean was not his usual self when he returned to their little room that evening. He had the look of a beaten man about him, which made Mary's heart ache.

After a supper of stew and bread, the two of them sat down by the fire. They had hardly spoken a word throughout the meal and now Mary felt she would be compounding his agony by telling him that there was no doubt Mallon knew about his scheme. But she needed to and it wouldn't be easy.

'But why should it worry Mallon if he was to lose you, Sean?' she asked.

'It would not be worry, Mary, just plain, cruel anger,' he replied. 'I don't know what he'd do.'

'What do you mean?' asked Mary fearfully.

'No one gives Mallon notice,' said Sean dully. 'He may give them the sack, but nobody leaves, especially if they know too much. Both men and women.'

'What would he do?'

'It's best not to talk about it,' replied Sean.

'I want to know!' cried Mary, taking his hands in hers.

'Can you not guess?'

'You mean . . . ?'

'Yes, I mean that our lives would not be worth a fig. I do not care for myself, but I do for you. I should never have allowed you to come here.'

116

'Don't say that, Sean!' cried Mary. 'Nor that you do not care what happens to you. We were going to get away anyway, weren't we?'

'We were but, if I had been able to speak to O'Mara, I might have known something about Mallon that would have stopped him from taking his usual course of action against us.' Mary did not dare to ask what such action was and if Sean himself had seen it all before. She could not bear to think that he might have been instrumental in getting rid of some of Mallon's enemies.

'What could O'Mara have told you?' she asked.

'In his first letter to me, he only said that he knew something about Mallon that would have changed things for me; that he could not write this knowledge down as it was far too dangerous if the letter had been intercepted.'

'You mean you were going to blackmail the boss,' said Mary, as if she was used to such crimes.

'I suppose so,' said Sean. 'And, now, the man is lying in the mortuary with a bullet in his back. Someone knows what news he could have imparted and that was why he was killed.'

'But who could that be?'

'The only person whom it would hurt, Mary. Mallon, of course!'

'You mean . . . that it was Mallon, who killed O'Mara?' asked Mary, shocked.

'I am sure that it was, but I have no proof.

He keeps a gun, Mary.' She knew that her face had gone pale. He caught her in his arms. 'Don't be afraid. I'll protect you,' he said, 'but, somehow, I have to find out if his gun is still where he usually hides it. He would not be stupid enough to keep it after a murder. He will have had it thrown in the river or something like that. He knows that however much he bribes O'Brien, sooner or later a higher authority will come looking for the weapon. He needs to be clean. He has powerful enemies, who are looking to clean up the streets of scum like Mallon.'

Mary was calm now, although her heart was beating fast. 'Where does he keep it, Sean?'

'His pistol is in a locked drawer in his office desk. It never leaves there. He uses it to protect himself. He never carries it on his person; if it was found on him, then he would be a suspect. If it is gone, then I shall have, at least, some proof that his secret is enough to kill for. And I can charge him with it.'

She knew what he was saying, what question he was asking, but couldn't bear to ask directly. She was the only one with direct access to Mallon's office.

'I could try to look,' she said, her face muffled against his shoulder.

'I can't ask you to do that, girleen,' he replied.

'You haven't asked me. I've offered,' she said. 'And, as you say, if it is not there, then he

118

has got rid of it, because he has a guilty conscience.'

'Thank you, Mary,' he replied and she heard his voice shake. 'I have been a bad lad in my time, but this is one of the worst things I have asked anyone to do, never mind a girl. All you need to do is get hold of his key. I'll do the rest.'

'But I am your girl,' she said bravely, disengaging herself from his embrace. 'You know I would do anything for you, Sean, because I love you.'

'That is what makes it worse,' he said 'I did not know what it was to love anyone before.'

'I know,' she replied, ruffling the front of his thick, dark hair, 'but now you do. Right, I'm going to get hold of the key to that drawer, I promise,' she said, doing her best to look brave.

'I know exactly where it is,' replied Sean, 'but I don't know how you can manage it. I feel really bad asking you to do this for me.'

'Not for me, for us,' corrected Mary. 'Now, tell me where he keeps it!'

CHAPTER TEN

Mary's heart was thudding as she stood outside Mallon's office at seven. She felt as if the secret plan was showing in her face already

119

as Katy passed her in the corridor, after a blowsy night with one of her customers.

'You're lucky, Mary Flynn, to be standing outside the master's door at this time in the morning. Some of us have been up all night.' Katy had never forgiven Mary for being so successful in what she referred to as 'netting Sean Mullen'.

'I know I am, Katy,' replied Mary gently but, that morning, she would have given anything not to be standing there ready to commit what Mallon would most surely call one of the 'crimes' perpetrated by his employees on whom he would bring down the full force of the law if he found out.

The girl passed by her with a poisonous look that Mary did not deserve. It was not her fault that Sean had fallen in love with her and was able to protect her from Katy's fate.

A moment later, she watched Mallon stride down the corridor towards her. He'd had a rough night himself by the look of it, he must have a guilty conscience if he had shot O'Mara. Sean seemed sure that he had been implicated and, now, it was Mary's task to find out if the gun was there, or if it had mysteriously disappeared.

As he approached, she asked herself what kind of man needed to protect himself with a firearm and was willing to use it on a defenceless fellow being.

He was still tucking his shirt in his trousers

120

as he reached her and he had the smell of drink about him even that early. 'So you managed to drag yourself out of Mullen's bed,' he sneered.

'Don't insult me, sir,' she said sharply, trying to calm herself inside. 'I said I would be on time.'

You want me to believe that young scamp is playing the gentleman, do you? More fool him,' replied Mallon dryly. 'I would not be so nice.'

Mary didn't answer but only thought to herself, No, you would not. Instead, she added, 'He is a gentleman, sir.' Mallon snorted and taking a bunch of keys out of his pocket, unlocked the office door.

As Mary stood patiently waiting for orders, she was going over what she had to do. She intended to start very soon. Sean had promised to be very near, from the moment she had entered the office.

'Will we be working together this morning, sir?' she asked.

'Why do you want to know?' Mallon seemed suspicious, as he unlocked one of the cupboards.

'I only asked because I found some of the accounts difficult. I hope I have done them correctly, sir.' Mary hoped that she was not staring too hard at him. She also had difficulty averting her eyes from the desk drawer, where the key she wanted lay.

'I checked them. I wouldn't have taken you on, Mary Flynn, if I had thought you were a donkey,' he replied nastily.

He turned, went over and sat down, then opened a couple of drawers and laid the bunch on the desk. Each of the keys had coloured tails, but no markings. Sean had told her that the red one was the one she needed. He leaned back. 'But a very pretty donkey,' he added.

She would not remonstrate whatever he said and waited until he thrust a sheaf of papers, covered in columns of numbers over to her. She took them and stared at them, then passed a hand over her forehead. He looked across.

Then she took a deep breath as if she was in pain. All the time, she was trying not to look at the red key. Letting out her breath, she gave a tiny moan. He looked up sharply again. 'What's the matter, girl?'

'Nothing, sir,' she replied, making a face.

'Are you in pain?'

'I often have this,' she lied. 'I don't know what it is but, at home, they told me that it was come from not having enough to eat.'

'What? Did your parents starve you?'

'Not starve,' she said carefully, thinking what a liar she had become and how much her mother would have been hurt should she have heard Mary. 'But we did not have a lot. Ah,' she leaned back, with her hand on her side just beneath her bosom. When they had concocted the plan, Sean had not been keen, in case Mallon had dared to investigate the pain, knowing his lewd temper.

'What did you get to eat this morning?' he asked. She could see he was falling into the trap. She had always been very good at making up stories to enthrall her audience, but she had never had such a dangerous one as Mallon. Mary knew she was playing with fire. She gasped once more with imaginary pain.

'Not much, sir, just toast and tea. I am thinking that this is caused from yesterday when Jimmy fetched the bagels—and I could not eat being put off by the sight in the street. So, as Sean was out later I went to bed hungry.'

'Aye, you look pale. That young divil is not looking after you, Mary. I know someone else who gladly would.' He grinned and got up from his chair. This was what Mary had both feared and hoped for.

As he came round and towards her, she uttered a piercing cry—her signal to Sean—and fell to the floor. She cringed, eyes shut, as Mallon bent over her, spilling his beery breath into her face.

'Mary!' he said, his hands on her. She almost fainted away for real then, but lay, feigning unconsciousness.

To her horror, he began loosening her top buttons, then put his ear to her mouth and, afterwards, chafed her wrists. Mary felt sick inside, but she had to go on for both Sean's sake and hers. Would he never go for help? They had calculated it would take him a good two minutes to find someone, as his office was isolated at the end of the corridor and he only slept in that area, away from prying eyes. It was a place where Mallon could do what he liked, to whom he liked. As he had probably done with Katy last night!

'Wake up, Mary, for God's sake,' he said. She did not respond. She lay motionless for what seemed an age and then, to her utter relief, she heard his heavy boots run across the room, the door open and him shouting, 'Help. Get up here, Paddy! Stir yourself, damn you! Help, anyone!'

A second later, Mary was on her feet, round the desk and, grabbing the red key, forced it into the lock, but her hands were shaking so much she couldn't do it. A moment later, Sean was beside her. He had been waiting in the shadow of a doorway outside.

He had it open in a second. 'No gun!' he said triumphantly. 'We have him, Mary.' They clung together in a split second embrace, then skittered apart as the door burst open with Mallon followed by Old Paddy, who knew a lot about doctoring.

'What's this,' spat Mallon. 'You young . . .' He stepped forward as if to strike out, but Sean grabbed him by the arm. 'It was you, then, who called for O'Mara!'

'Lose yourself, Paddy!' Sean ordered and the old man was gone like a frightened rabbit.

'What do you think you're up to? I'll have the police on you for this.' Mallon was staring at the desk drawer.

'Yes, the gun's gone! And you've just admitted that you knew O'Mara was here to tell me something,' snarled Sean. Mary had never seen such a look on his face. It frightened her. His expression almost the same as the one on Mallon's. 'Sit down, Mallon!'

'Make me!' shouted his boss. 'You'll pay for this with a nice, long term in jail. And so will your sweetheart!' Mary shivered. 'You're after my money, is it? And she knows where it is now.'

'We don't want your money,' growled Sean. Mallon had wrested out of Sean's grasp and was edging towards the desk. 'Did you forget the gun has gone?' Mallon stopped. Mary had never seen anything like the look on his face. 'I need no gun. I will take up my fists and break you, Sean Mullen.'

'You will not,' said Sean.

Mary gasped. 'Don't fight him, Sean. Tell him what you want,' she cried.

'I don't need to fight him,' replied Sean, his hand darting inside his coat. A moment later, Mary saw the glittering pistol.

'No, Sean, no. Please, no. If you do this, you'll be as bad as he is.' She couldn't bear the thought.

'She's right, lad,' stuttered Mallon, backing off.

Sean took no notice. 'Stand away, Mary,' he said. 'This is between me and him. I will have the truth out of him. Whatever it takes.'

'No, please, Sean,' begged Mary, withdrawing. She didn't know what to do. She had never expected Sean owned a gun as well. Suddenly, she was terrified that he might use it—and then their future together was over.

Suddenly, he was forcing Mallon back towards the desk. 'Get down on your knees,' he ordered, 'and beg for your life. You have this coming to you for all you have made me do.'

'Then don't add murder to your list,' snarled Mallon, white-faced.

'Like you, you mean,' retorted Sean madly. He brought the gun close to Mallon's face. 'You killed O'Mara, didn't you?'

'You've gone mad,' replied Mallon, but he looked shocked.

'Guilt is all over your face,' said Sean, who had suddenly become calm. Mary had never heard such coldness in any voice, let alone the man she had come to love. She swallowed back words that had sprung into her head. Throw down the gun, Sean. We can go. Come with me. It will be all right. But it never would be any more if Sean killed the man cowering in front of him.

'You threw away the gun! Where is it? Lying

in the harbour, I'll be bound.'

'Why would I want to kill someone I'd never seen before?' Mallon blustered.

'You're a liar, and I am going to get the truth out of you this time. You knew him all right. What had O'Mara got to say to me that you didn't want me to hear? Answer me!' At that, he rammed the pistol barrel against Mallon's temple. Mary closed her eyes. She felt sick. What if Mallon wouldn't answer? But he did.

'Take away the gun. You wouldn't want to kill me, Sean.'

'Wouldn't I?' persisted Sean grimly, without moving a muscle.

'If you kill me, you'll always regret it,' Mallon said in the quietest voice Mary had ever heard him use. 'I promise you, lad, I'm speaking the truth this time.'

'You will die, if you don't.'

'Mary, make him see sense,' Mallon hissed.

'She will not, for I am more sensible than I have ever been. I should have killed you when you first took me in to this place,' Sean replied. 'For it has been a miserable life, doing for you what you could not do yourself.'

'Don't you think that is why I chose you for it?' replied Mallon. Sean lowered the gun a little, but Mary could see he wasn't weakening.

'I had never stolen nor hurt a soul until I met you.'

'Do you know why that is, lad?' retorted

127

Mallon, adjusting his neck tie. A moment later, Sean was close up to him with the gun once more. 'Because I saw in you what is in me. You have a hardness—a way of getting things done, the determination to yourself.'

'This won't help you,' replied Sean dangerously.

'No, but it might help you.'

'I don't need your help, just the truth. Why did you murder O'Mara?'

'If I tell you, Sean, will you swear not to kill me afterwards?'

'Sean wouldn't do that!' burst out Mary.

'I want to hear him promise,' cried Mallon.

'How will I know you're speaking the truth—if I promise?'

'You will, when you hear what I have to say,' said Mallon. 'Will you let me sit down? If you are really set on murdering me, I would like to die in my chair.' Sean gestured his agreement by waving the gun.

A second later, Mallon slipped into his chair, white-faced and leaned back with Sean behind him.

'I don't want to die with a bullet in my back,' he said.

'You blackguard,' replied Sean. 'That is how O'Mara died.'

'I am sorry for it.'

'Huh. You don't know what sorrow means,' Sean retorted.

'I do,' replied Mallon. 'I have not always

been this way. I have grown hard. I have had to make some hard decisions.'

'Stop whingeing and tell me about O'Mara!'

'He used to frequent this place . . .'

'That's not news to me,' persisted Sean grimly. 'He was coming to see me, as you guessed. What had he to say that made you kill him—or have him killed? What did he know about you?'

Mary held her breath. How much longer could Sean keep his temper? Suddenly, she wanted to fly at him and wrest the gun from his grasp, but if she did, they would still be lost. Mallon would have the police on them and then it would all be over just the same.

'What didn't you want me to know?' he persisted.

'It depends on what you wanted to know from him,' replied Mallon. 'What did you want to know?' Sean was silent for what seemed ages.

Mary couldn't stand it. 'For God's sake, Sean, tell him,' she cried. He remained silent.

'I think I know what he wanted,' added Mallon, who was looking braver now, but even paler. 'But he's stubborn.' Mary had to admire his courage, if one could call it that. Rather foolhardiness, seeing the position he was in. 'He wanted to know about his father. O'Mara knew the man well. So do I. Too well.

'He wanted to know what kind of a man he was. Well, I'll tell you then. He's a man like

129

Sean himself. As he should be, he has handed a great deal of himself over to his son. A proud man, who does not want to think about the past. Of the things he has done. Of the tears he has caused. Of the sadness. A man, who should never have . . .' Mallon stopped. Sean was staring at him, while Mary stared at them both.

'What are you talking about? Where is my father? Is he still here? If he is, I want to find the blackguard,' burst out Sean.

'And you have found him,' said Mallon wearily. 'He is sitting in this chair, waiting for you to end his miserable life.' He gave a great sigh then, and passed a hand over his eyes, then leaned forward, to put his head in his hands.

Mary and Sean gaped at each other then, to her horror, Mary saw Sean lift the gun deliberately and point it at Mallon's head. 'You liar,' he said quietly and Mary's heart almost burst for the broken way he spoke.

'Don't, Sean, don't!' she screamed. 'Can't you see he's speaking the truth. It all adds up. He's just like . . .' She realised what she was going to say. Sean looked at her dumbly. 'I don't mean you're like him, but in some ways I can see a resemblance. No! Don't go mad. There are gestures and signs and . . .'

She didn't know how to explain what she was making such a mess of saying to them both.

'Let him kill me, Mary,' Mallon muttered. 'I deserve it. I tried to keep it from him. To make him hard, so he wouldn't care. So he'd survive . . .'

'Shut your mouth!' shouted Sean. At that moment, Mary grabbed the gun and Sean let her take it. She had never held a pistol before and it weighed heavy in her hand. Mary stared at the ugly weapon in disgust, but kept on holding it.

A second later, Sean had jumped on Mallon and was thumping and pummelling his back with his fists. Mallon bent lower and lower, without a murmur. When Sean stopped, he lay, motionless, face down on the desk.

'You've killed him, Sean, you've killed him,' Mary cried, distraught.

'I have not. I have only beaten him within an inch of his life. I thrashed him and he deserved it,' replied Sean, flinging his arms round her and, suddenly, he was sobbing against her shoulder, like a little child. So Mary held him and the gun, letting him cry it out.

When he had recovered, they both went over to Mallon and turned him over. He was not dead, as Sean had said but, when they raised his head, he could hardly speak for coughing. When he could, he was a sorry sight with blood dripping from out of the corners of his mouth. He groaned.

By then, they could hear other noises

outside. Mary quickly concealed the pistol inside her skirts, while Mallon dumbly waved his hand towards Sean, who went over to the door and opened it and was confronted by half a dozen terrified faces, including Old Paddy's and little Jimmy's.

'Everything is all right now. The boss and I have been having an argument.' They peered in and Mallon waved them away. A moment later, they scuttled off like frightened animals.

'Don't think you're getting off that easy,' Sean said, grimly, now he had recovered himself. 'I want to know everything from you. And I want the truth!'

CHAPTER ELEVEN

'Don't think I shall ever forgive you,' said Sean, in an icy voice as Mallon loosened is neck tie, straightened his waistcoat and swallowed half a glass of spirit. Mary had found the bottle in one of the many cupboards and poured out a glass for him.

Sean had refused any drink so that his head would be clear. 'And make sure you speak no lies, or I'll give you some more,' he added.

Mary had offered to leave while they talked, but Sean wouldn't let her so she sat down in relief. She was still holding the gun, but felt better now as she believed fervently that Sean would never murder his own father.

Mallon took a deep breath in and the one that came out, rasped, 'I changed my name to Mallon, from Mullen—it took just two letters. I came over from Ireland and ended up at The Shamrock, where nobody knew me. Except for O'Mara. He had come over on the boat with me and, like you, Sean, became my companion in crime, until he couldn't take it any more and left for a job in Boston where he became respectable.'

'And you killed him!' Sean glared.

Mallon ignored the intervention and continued, 'He was no angel. Those who live by the sword perish by the sword.' Mary stared.

'Don't bother to quote the Holy Bible, you hypocrite, just get on with it,' ordered Sean. 'I want to know what made you leave Ireland— and your infant.'

'Mary might be interested in what I am about to say. I was very interested in her, when I heard where she came from. As were you, were you not, my son!'

'Don't call me that!' snapped Sean.

'What does he mean?' asked Mary. Mallon was the one to answer.

'Sean found out you were from Brala, my dear, which made you very interesting. After all, he knew where his mother came from. The ladies, with whom he was left, told him his history, omitting, of course, any details of that

133

scoundrel, his wastrel father!'

'Mary, don't look like that,' said Sean. 'Come over here.' She did—and sat by him. He whispered, 'It just seemed like heaven when I heard where you came from, the place of my dreams.' She believed him totally.

'I don't understand, what you just said, Mallon,' cried Mary.

'You will,' said Mallon. 'Doubtless, Sean told you he was some kind of lord?' Sean was glaring again. 'The seal you sent to The Shamrock?'

Mary nodded. She understood how he had got to see it. Like he saw everything that came or went. 'Did you never see its like before?' Mary frowned. She remembered that tiny glimmer of recognition she'd had on the boat when Sean first showed it to her. 'The Brala arms?' Where had she seen them?

'What?' She was utterly astonished as she finally remembered—it was carved on a weatherbeaten old shield, that stood over the front door to the Big House. But what did it have to do with all this?

'Lord and Lady Bennett,' said Mallon. 'How I hated his lordship, arrogant devil that he was! Did you never hear a whisper of scandal from there, Mary?'

'I did not,' said Mary, affronted, but she knew she had.

'I forget you're a good Catholic girl.'

Mary blushed. She had not been to Mass for

134

months, nor seen a priest. 'Leave her alone. Save your nastiness for me,' hissed Sean.

'I have done you all the disservice I could,' replied Mallon brazenly. 'Besides Mary is a Flynn and I am very fond of Flynns.' Mary swallowed. What was he going to say next, but she could hardly concentrate as she was trying to remember the bits of scandal she had heard about the Big House. 'Sean didn't tell you that either, how I came to know Brala?' Mary shook her head, hoping she wasn't going to cry.

It had begun to dawn on her that maybe, just maybe, Sean Mullen had got to know her on the boat for his own sake. He had asked her so many questions. But then she told herself that wasn't true, because he loved her. Mallon's next sentence was even more shocking than what had gone before.

'I knew your dadda, Mary. Conor Flynn!'

'How could you?' She almost screamed. Her dadda was the best of men. He would never have done anything like Mallon, nor even have anything to do with a man like him.

'Don't worry, Mary. He was a good, upright fellow, your father—and I was a rogue from birth. But that didn't stop me having friends. He was a good friend to me, your dadda. When we were both turned off our land, he got a job at Brala before I did and, afterwards, had me brought over to work in the gardens and with the horseflesh. He was not a man for betting, whereas I am. And I am betting now, that you are already suspecting my son of something underhand, which I tell you is not possible for Sean is a good lad too, even though he has some of me about him.'

'Be quiet,' Sean thundered.

'I thought you wanted to hear the truth,' said Mallon nastily. Mary could never think of Mallon as ever being a Mullen and having anything to do with Sean.

'Such a thing has never come into my mind!' Mary replied stoutly.

'You've a good, loyal girl there, son!' pronounced Mallon, then caught Sean's warning glance. 'Yes, I came to Brala on the advice and good efforts of Conor Flynn and, then, I let him down. In fact, I let myself down. And her.' He stopped, as if he couldn't bear to go on.

'Get on with it!' growled Sean, getting up. Mallon took the hint and shrunk back in his chair. 'I fell in love. Which is a thing that happens, does it not?' He looked first at Mary, then at Sean. 'Now you know what it's like.'

'Don't compare our love with yours,' remarked Sean bitterly.

'But I was young then. And my feelings for your mother were true. At the time.' Mallon defended himself stubbornly.

'My mother was a married woman,' said Sean coldly. 'And, yet, you made a play for her.' Mary gasped. The story about Lady

136

Bennett and the unknown child was coming back to her. But everyone said that the baby she was carrying had died. The old gossips had added, that it was the best for everyone. That baby had been Sean! She could hardly believe it.

'Begging pardon, Sean, the lady was as much in love with me as I was her. And I was a simple groom in her stables. She was not getting what she wanted from my lord and . . .'

'Shut up!' warned Sean.

'So you don't want to hear the truth?'

'I do, but no slander on my mother's name. You seduced her.'

'And she let me!' said Mallon stoutly. It was as if he was trying to antagonise Sean further. 'I would have married her.'

'If she had not been married!' Sean burst out scornfully. 'You behaved like a cad.' Mallon nodded.

'I did, indeed. And I have paid for it. I lost her and you. Our affair was hushed up. I was discharged with a boot up my backside and not a penny to my name. And look what I have now.'

He gestured at the room around him. 'I have done well. And so have you.'

'You call this well? Depriving me of my mother and letting me grow up with a family who were not mine. I was the butt of jokes. A by-blow. No one knew from where I came, but they all knew really.' Sean's tone was so bitter that Mary's heart went out to him.

'You were fed and clothed well. Better than any other child in your village.'

'Aye. By my mother, who sent the money to assuage her guilt and yours. But I never knew who she was, until I was leaving Ireland and the ladies in the family told me and gave me the address of the Shamrock Tree. It was then I resolved to find you and make you pay for what you did to me.'

'When I got over here and started to make my way in the world, I sent letters to your family, via this place.'

'Unsigned. With no personal address. What kind of letters were those?'

'Better than none. Many men, better than I, use this address. And many women.' Mallon said, brazening it out. Mary flushed. She had done the same. Written to the Shamrock Tree not knowing what kind of place it was and who would be there.

'And, now, you've found me, what are you going to do?' Sean's lips were set in a straight, hard line. 'You are not going to kill me, are you?'

'Maybe.'

'Sean, you can't,' cried Mary. 'He's your father.'

'He's been no father to me. He means nothing to me.'

'I know that, but I have taught you my trade,' sneered Mallon. Mary rushed forward

138

as Sean put up his fists.

'Stop, Sean, stop. Stop and think. We can get away now. If we leave him alone, he'll not set the police on us and you'll never have to see him any more.'

'Listen to her, son,' said Mallon. 'She's right as a good woman usually is. I will furnish you with money, so you will not leave empty-handed. Enough to get you where you want to go.'

'Maybe I'll go to the police myself and report you,' replied Sean stubbornly.

'No, Sean,' cried Mary again. 'They may not believe you. It will be his word against yours. You have no proof that he is your father.'

'Then I have to get rid of him.' Sean's look frightened her. And it seemed to frighten Mallon.

'Maybe you won't be so eager to kill me when you hear the rest.'

'And what is that?' asked Sean coldly. Mallon went to open one of the drawers, but Sean darted forward and imprisoned him in a strangling arm lock.

'Sean, don't!' commanded Mary. 'You'll break his neck.' She drew the gun out. It felt extremely light in her hand. 'I will point this at him, while he shows us.' Sean let Mallon go, surprise in his face and stepped towards her, leaving his father moaning and rubbing his shoulders. 'No, I will do it.' She moved the gun away from Sean's grasp. 'I think we have had enough brutality today.'

'Bravo, little Mary,' gasped Mallon. He went for the drawer and opened it.

'He might have another gun!' shouted Sean. 'Watch out, Mary!' But, instead, Mallon drew out a bundle of letters and threw them on the desk.

'These are from your mother,' he said. 'Go on. Look at them. They came addressed to you. Most of them are old. The top two or three have arrived in the last six months.'

'God forgive you!' said Sean, grabbing them. He looked at Mary, as if he didn't know what to do.

'Open them,' urged Mary. Sean collapsed into the chair and stared at them, then took the top one and opened it. Mary sat down opposite the two of them, still holding the gun . . .

What she intended to do with it then, she didn't know but, months later, she remembered that day Sean faced up to Mallon, as one of the worst—and the best—in her life. After that, one day seemed to melt into another, until the morning came when Sean and she left The Shamrock Tree behind and took ship for home.

CHAPTER TWELVE

'You were very brave on that day, Mary,' Sean said, pulling his arm closely about her waist. They'd had good weather all the way across the Atlantic and it seemed as if God was smiling on them. That morning they were strolling on the deck they felt like two lovers, who hadn't a care in the world.

'I don't think so,' she replied doubtfully, 'but don't let's talk about the past any more, Sean. We must look to the future.' That was a phrase Lady Bennett had used in her letter.

It had been almost too good to believe, although Mary knew she ought not to be rejoicing in Lord Bennett's death. He had been killed in the hunting field, which was a fitting, although horrible end for a man, who did little else but chase foxes and stags and who treated his servants with equal disdain.

Lady Bennett had never loved him, or so it seemed. The English lord had come to Ireland looking for a well-off Irish lady to marry and her father had a fancy to have a noble name in the family. So the old traitor had married her off.

In the letter to Sean, she'd owned up to loving the man, who had deserted her and his illegitimate son, who was now being punished for all his crimes.

Mary and Sean had no part in Michael Mallon's arrest, as the police were already on his trail as Sean said they would be. A witness had come forward, who swore he had seen the felonious act and who, after being promised a tidy sum and a safe dispatch out of New York, had identified Mallon as O'Mara's assassin. So Mallon's own sanctimonious words about his victim had now been turned on himself: Those who live by the sword, die by the sword.

One thing Mary was sad about, but could understand, was Sean's utter refusal to go and see his father in jail. She hoped that, finally, he might come to terms with this. But he had not.

Afterwards, the two of them were free to do what they liked. Marry even! Sean had written to his mother and, since then, letters had been exchanged and, on Lady Bennett's side, came the express wish that Sean should return to Brala and take up his place as her rightful heir.

She'd had several obstacles to overcome, seeing that the title died with my lord. But Lady Bennett had been the Irish woman who had owned the land, in her own right until she'd married and become his property. Now he was dead, she was free to bestow her land on whoever she wished.

Mary had always been a favourite with Lady Bennett as had her father. Now she knew why. She had been a little frightened when she and Sean had written to his mother to tell her that they had met in New York and fallen in love,

142

and that they wished to return to Ireland together.

Lady Bennett's reply had been as Mary had hoped. Yes, it did seem like a miracle, but it was clearly meant to be.

Mary wondered with some little satisfaction how her stepfather had taken the news. Now she would be the important one and would be able to look after her mother as she had wanted. Besides, she had some money of her own now.

Her Aunt Flynn had perished in that terrible fire, but she had been a business woman and left a tidy sum in life insurance, which had been made over to the niece, with whom she had hoped to share her life.

It all seemed too good to be true and, here they were today, standing on the deck. They had taken passage as a lady and gentleman would and had quarters next to each other, far above those they had shared in steerage, when they had come over to America as poor emigrants.

'No hauling of ropes today, Sean?' said Mary, looking across the deck at the sailors at work. She was holding on to her hat fast, in case it blew away.

'No hiding away from me in a bunk,' he said, that impudent look he'd worn then, now replaced by a soft expression she had grown to love.

'Sean, did you make a friend of me at first,

143

because I came from Brala?'

'I would be telling you a lie, if I said that it had not made you of extra interest. But I was netted by those blue eyes of yours already,' he said. 'When I heard you came from Brala, I couldn't believe my luck. I think . . .' She had never seen him lost for words, except for the time he took hold of those precious letters.

'Yes?' she probed gently.

'. . . I think that I have been searching for love all of my life. Until I met you. Then I knew I had found it.'

'Do you know, Sean, I feel exactly the same,' she replied comfortably, turning her face to him. Seconds later, Mary felt his strong lips on hers and his arms about her. Which she knew was the place they must always be. His search was over. As was hers.